I0614729

John Duncan Hilarius Dale

The Sacristan's manual

Or handbook of church furniture, ornament, etc.

John Duncan Hilarius Dale

The Sacristan's manual
Or handbook of church furniture, ornament, etc.

ISBN/EAN: 9783741192135

Manufactured in Europe, USA, Canada, Australia, Japa

Cover: Foto ©Andreas Hilbeck / pixelio.de

Manufactured and distributed by brebook publishing software
(www.brebook.com)

John Duncan Hilarius Dale

The Sacristan's manual

THE

SACRISTAN'S MANUAL;

OR,

Hand-Book of Church Furniture, Ornament, &c.

HARMONIZED WITH

THE MOST APPROVED COMMENTARIES ON THE ROMAN CEREMONIAL,

AND THE

LATEST DECREES OF THE SACRED CONGREGATION OF RITES

BY THE

REV. J. D. HILARIUS DALE.

"Ubi Petrus, ibi Ecclesia."—St. Ambrose.

THIRD EDITION, GREATLY ENLARGED.

LONDON:

T. BOOKER, 53, NEW BOND STREET.

ADVERTISEMENT TO THE THIRD EDITION.

FOLLOWING the advice of many of his kind friends, the Author has, in this Edition, given the measurements of the Sacred Vestments from those which are now in common use in Rome, and not, as in the First Edition, from the treatise of Gavantus. He has also given the preparations to be made for the Functions of the various seasons of the year *in full;* so that, in this respect, the Sacristan will be no longer under the necessity of referring to his larger work, "The Ceremonial according to the Roman Rite." An Appendix, on the cultivation of flowers in room-windows for the Altars, and some occasional matter, have also been added. Since the publication of the former Edition, the Author has again visited Rome, and no pains have been spared to make his little work worthy of the kind patronage bestowed upon it.

PREFACE.

THE object of the present Manual is not merely to give such practical rules as will enable the lay Sacristan to fulfil the duties of his office with ease and method, but also to furnish that information of a higher order concerning matters which relate to the care of the Church and its sacred appurtenances, which is more or less necessary, that the sacred ceremonies of the Church may be carried out according to the rule of Rome.

To enable those of the Clergy intrusted with the externals of religion to refer to the authorities cited, a list of the editions of those works which the Author has consulted is given at the end of the Preface. The decrees of the Sacred Congregation of Rites may be found in the *Manuale Ecclesiasticorum* and other collections; in minor points, where the date is not given, they may be referred to by means of the indexes of those works.

The plan pursued throughout the Manual has been, first, to insist upon that which is laid down in the Liturgical Books, as the Rubrics of the Missal, the Ceremonial of Bishops, &c.; secondly, where these are silent, to take the opinions of approved commentators on the Roman Rite, as Catalani, Gavantus, and others; and, lastly, where these fail, the practice and custom of Rome. Such is undoubtedly suggested by the Council of Westminster. In the 26th Decree (No. 5), after recommending, for the sake of uni-

formity, the use of the Roman plain chant, it goes on to
say: "Orationes ergo, responsoria, epistola, evangelium et
alia hujusmodi, prout in Cæremoniali episcoporum, vel in
aliis authenticis libris traditur, canantur. Idem dicendum
de rubricis, et cæremoniis ecclesiasticis; in quibus non pro
lubito adoptandæ consuetudines aliarum nationum, sed ad-
hærendum stricte definitionibus et regulis, et, his defici-
entibus, usibus et praxi S. Romanæ Ecclesiæ."

It is as well here to state, that that which is given as
Roman custom has been for the most part taken from
written notes, made by the Author during his residence in
Rome, at the time he was engaged translating the larger
treatise of Baldeschi, and had his attention constantly
called to the various subjects incidental to a study of the
Ceremonial.

It may not be inappropriate to add a few words of
admonition to Lay Sacristans. They occupy a rank in the
Church which is next only to that of the Clergy themselves. Hence, where such an arrangement is practicable,
and where the Church has her will and her way without
drawback, the Sacristan is a Priest, or at least in Orders.
The Pope's Sacristan is a Bishop—a fact which may be
taken as an indication of the importance which the Church
attaches to this office. A little thought will show the
reasonableness of this estimate of the Sacristan's duties.
In the course of his labours he is brought constantly, and
closely, near the Altar of God and the Holy of Holies. He
is almost necessitated to touch the Sacred vessels and linen;
wherefore, if he have not this right *ex ordine,* he usually
receives it *ex officio.* The privileges, of which this is but a
specimen, are very great and very serious. No one can live
in the midst of them and remain the man he was when he
entered upon them. No man can be near God without a

blessing or a curse. The familiarity with sacred things is, of all habits, the most dangerous where it is not duly appreciated, and its temptations constantly foreseen and counteracted. It is commonly said by Priests, that Altar-boys end in being either angels or the reverse. Now, the first duty of a Sacristan is to weigh the importance of his duties; and it is hoped that even so trifling an effort as the present may lead. to this result, by pointing out the necessity of care and cleanliness in all that relates to the Church, and that hence, by the blessing of God, it may indirectly further the ends of personal sanctification.

The habits which every Sacristan has most need to cultivate are :—

1. *Cleanliness.*—No words can overrate the importance of this habit. Cleanliness is the very outward expression of the beauty of sanctity; and while no exterior magnificence can supply its place, *it* is alone sufficient to give propriety and attractiveness to the simplest worship in the meanest building. It need scarcely be added, that personal cleanliness on the part of the Sacristan himself is of the first importance towards the habit of cleanliness in his work.

2. *Forethought.*—No one requires more than the Sacristan to have all his eyes and all his wits about him. Church ceremonial is one of those matters in which no mere *habit* secures a person against mistakes, without habitual *advertence.* The good Sacristan, therefore, will forecast in his mind all the circumstances of each service he has to perform; run over in it the progress of the ceremonial, and imagine every possible want which may arise, with the view of providing against it. Nothing is more disturbing, both to priest and to congregation, than to see attendants running backwards and forwards during a solemnity. All

parties, indeed, have need of forbearance, for, as the saying goes, "in the best-regulated families accidents will happen;" still it is in the power of *forethought* (especially in the Sacristan) to guard indefinitely against these mishaps.

3. *Interest in his Duties.*—This facilitates and effectuates every work; but in a Sacristan, whose functions are so unspeakably important, the want of it is fatal to success. There is nothing in these functions to interest any one, *except* their religious character; and this, if it interest at all, must interest in the highest degree.

4. *Good Temper.*—No office is more trying to the temper than that of the Sacristan. He has to deal with all kinds of people, and is often drawn twenty ways at once. He will frequently fall upon those who are unreasonable in their expectations, and wish him to do things which are not his business. Even then, however, he must answer with mildness, self-possession, and forbearance. A great help to this end will be,

5. *Method,* which will prevent his being ever *hurried,* and so, excited. To these qualities may be added others connected with them, such as diligence, punctuality, courtesy to strangers, &c. &c. But the first qualification of all, and that which is the guarantee for all the rest, is a true spirit of devotion to God in his work, and the habitual use of practices which tend to keep it alive and active.

In conclusion, the Author has but to add that he will feel much obliged to Priests, or experienced Sacristans, if they will make any suggestions by which this little work may be rendered worthier of its subject and of the encouragement which has called it forth.

J. D. H. DALE.

LIST OF
ABBREVIATIONS AND AUTHORITIES CITED.

———◆◆———

Bald.—Baldeschi.—Esposizione delle Sacre Cerimonie, Roma, 1848.

Bar.—Baruffaldi.—Ad Rituale Romanum Commentaria, Venetiis, 1792.

Benedict XIV.—Institutiones Ecclesiasticæ, Lovanii, 1762 ; Bullarium, Mech-
liniæ, 1827.

Bisso.—Hierurgia, sive Rei Divinæ Peractio, Genes, 1686.

Cær. Ep.—The Ceremonial of Bishops.

Catalani.—Sacra·um Cæremoniarum, sive Rituum Ecclesiasticorum Sacræ
Romanæ Ecclesiæ libri tres, commentariis aucti ; 2 vol. in fol. Romæ,
1750.

Cavalieri.—Opera omnia Liturgica, seu Commentaria, &c. Romæ, 1764.

Clement Instr.—The Clementine Instructions.

Conc. West.—The Provincial Council of Westminster.

Corsetti.—Praxis Sacrorum Rituum et Cæremoniarum ; 3 vol. in 12mo.
Venetiis, 1739.

Fornici.—Instit. Liturg, Paris, 1852.

Gardellini.—Decreta authentica Cong. Sac. Rit. ex actis ejusdem S. Con-
gregationis collecta, Romæ, 1824—1850.

Gav.—Gavantus.—Thesaurus Sacrorum Rituum ; 5 vol. in 4to. Venetiis,
1823.

Manuale Episc.—Manual for the use of Bishops, given in the fifth vol. of
Gavantus.

Merati.—The Rubrician who has given the above edition of Gavantus, with
notes, &c.

Rit. Rom.—The Roman Ritual.

Rubr. Miss.—The Rubrics of the Missal.

S. C. Episc.—Scilicet, Congregatio Card. super Negotia Episcoporum, et
Regul.

S. C. R.—The Sacred Congregation of Rites.

TABLE OF CONTENTS.

PART I.

THE SACRISTIES AND CHURCH.

PART II.

GENERAL PREPARATIONS FOR THE DIVINE OFFICES.

PART III.

PREPARATIONS FOR THE VARIOUS SEASONS OF THE YEAR.

APPENDIX I.

APPENDIX II.

APPENDIX III.

SACRISTAN'S MANUAL.

PART I.

THE SACRISTIES AND CHURCH.

ARTICLE I.—*The Sacristies.*

1. THE Sacristies should be furnished with presses for the vestments, &c., according to the requirements of the Church. In Italy there are sometimes as many presses as Altars in the Church; each, being supplied with complete sets of vestments, is appropriated to one particular Altar. One press, not less than 9 feet long, should be placed directly opposite the door leading into the Church or outer Sacristy, for the Celebrant and his Ministers to vest at for the more solemn functions. Each press should have a platform before it, about 4 feet wide and 6 inches high, as the Clergy when vesting should be raised a step above the ordinary level of the floor.—*Baldeschi.*—The Sacristies of some Churches have long continuous presses, having sufficient space for the number of Altars, the centre position being reserved for the solemn functions.

The presses should be about 3 feet wide, and 3 feet 5 inches high from the platform; they should be fitted with shallow drawers, some of them not more than sufficient to hold one set of vestments; for nothing tends to injure the vestments so much as tumbling the uppermost over to get at those underneath. The drawers should, if possible, be lined with cedar, to keep out insects ; some few should again be lined with cloth or baize dyed in saffron, which preserves gold embroidery-work : these latter will necessarily be reserved for the more costly vestments.   The drawers should be protected in front by folding, or, if possible, as more convenient, by *sliding* doors.   Green baize is a con-venient material for the cover of the presses, as it may easily be kept clean with a hard brush, and wax or other substance likely to soil the vestments may easily be detected. Some few feet above the centre press there should be a bracket fixed to the wall, upon which the crucifix is placed. It is allowed to replace the crucifix with a picture or an image ; usually, where the latter is the case, the Patron Saint of the Church is substituted.   A smaller press, con-taining small cupboards for the chalices, and drawers for the purificators, is sometimes conveniently placed on the centre of the vestment-press behind : in this case the crucifix or image may stand upon it.   Small wooden pegs, placed within these cupboards, on which the purificators may be hung, are preferred to drawers, as it enables the puri-ficators to dry better.   The names of the Priests of the mission should be written over the pegs, that each may have his own.

The other presses or cupboards required in a well-regu-lated Sacristy, will be mentioned under the heads of the respective articles to be kept in them.

St. Charles Borromeo in his instructions on Ecclesiastical Buildings recommends, where practicable, that there should be a recess, or small chamber, suitably provided with an Altar, to which the Clergy may retire for prayer and recol-lection.   In order also that the Sacristy may be unencum-bered and free from obstructions, he would have some place, or room, near at hand, in which may be deposited such things as the Bier, funeral candlesticks, stands for crosses, tenebræ candlesticks, etc., etc.   A most desirable addition to the modern Sacristy is a fire-proof iron safe embedded in the wall, and fitted with an additional outer door of panel-work.   This should have two or more com-partments in which the plate, deeds, and other valuables of the Church may be safely deposited.

2. *The Vestments* are divided into two classes,—sacred and ordinary. The sacred vestments are the chasuble, cope, stole, maniple, dalmatic, tunic, and humeral veil. When spoken of under the term " sacred ornaments " (*paramenta sacra*), the veil of the chalice, burse, antependium of the Altar, and veil of the Tabernacle, are to be included. The ordinary vestments, or those not called sacred, are the alb, cotta, amice, girdle, &c.

3. *The Sacred Ornaments* are to be assimilated in shape to those in use at Rome.[1] Each will presently be spoken of under its own name. The colours used by the Church are white, red, purple, green, and black. Cloth of gold is allowed to be used for all colours except black and purple. —*S. C. R.* All the sacred ornaments may be trimmed with gold, and especially is this fitting in the case of black vestments, on which the Rubric of the Ceremonial of Bishops (lib. 2, cap. xi., n. 1.) does not allow white crosses or mortuary devices.

Neither blue nor yellow is allowed ;[2] nor is it permitted to intermix colours with a view to use one set of vestments for either white, red, or green.[3]

4. The material of the sacred ornaments should be silk ;[1] cloth of gold or silver may be freely used, but glass-cloth, linen, printed muslin, or calico, is strictly prohibited.— *S. C. R.* The linings may be of a less costly material, but a plain silk should by all means be preferred to merino or calico.

5. The whole of the sacred vestments are to be blessed by the Bishop, or Priest having authority to do so.

6. It is recommended never to use the chasubles belonging to complete High-Mass sets for Low Masses, as the

---

[1] Paramenta sacra ex holoserico, reliquæ vestes et tobaleæ altaris ex solo lino conficiantur. Ut vero uniformitas hisce in rebus obtineat, adlaborandum est ut forma paramentorum sacrorum usui Ecclesiæ Romanæ accommodetur. —*Conc. West.* decret. xviii. n. 1.

[2] Utrum liceat uti colore flavo vel cæruleo in sacrificio missæ, et expositione SS. Sacramenti ? Resp. *negative.—S. R. C. die Martii*, 1833.

[3] Num paramenta confecta ex serico, et aliis coloribus floribusque intertexta, ita ut vix dignoscatur color primarius et prædominans, usurpari valeant mixtim saltem pro albo, rubro et viridi ? Resp. *negative.—*23 Sept., 1837.

extra wear will cause them to look shabby in contrast with
the dalmatic and tunic at Solemn Mass. A complete set of
purple vestments will include two extra chasubles, and the
stolone or large stole. Black humeral veils, or black veils
for the Tabernacle, are not required.

7. Vestments of cloth of gold and embroidery should
not be wrapped in common white silver-paper; Chinese
curling-paper is preferable, and unbleached calico dipped
in a decoction of saffron better than either. To prevent
creases being left in the more costly vestments, rolls of
wool padding of various lengths may be placed in the folds.
It is recommended to place in the drawers amongst the
vestments not frequently used, small bags containing lumps
of camphor, or chips of sandal-wood. The latter may be
purchased at the drysalter's.

8. *Chasuble*, to be about 2 feet 5 inches wide and 3 feet
6 or 7 inches long, with the pillar behind and Cross in front,
each about $9\frac{3}{4}$ inches wide, inclusive of the stripes of lace,
which should be $1\frac{1}{8}$ inches wide. Tapes or ribbons to be
so fastened underneath, that the chasuble may be securely
tied before the breast.—*Gav.*

9. *Stole,* to be about 6 feet 8 inches long, inclusive of
fringe, and about $4\frac{1}{2}$ inches wide; the fringe at the ends to
be about $2\frac{1}{4}$ inches wide. The stole has three crosses, one
on the middle, and the others at the ends. The Deacon's
stole to have two cords with tassels.—*Gav.*

Gardellini says that the stole is not a sign of jurisdiction
for Bishops, much less for Priests; it is only to be considered a vestment of honour, which should be worn by
Priests when exercising certain functions either in their
own character, or by delegation from another. The Sacred
Congregation of Rites has many times declared that the
stole ought only to be worn for celebrating Mass, for
administering the Sacraments, and on other occasions
when the Rubrics declare it to be necessary, which is understood of those various ceremonies called *Sacramentals*. It
is upon these principles, continues Gardellini, that the parish
Priest does not wear the stole when he is not officiating, or
when he merely assists in his own church at a baptism or
marriage administered by another priest. Also upon the

same principles he does not wear it when assisting the Bishop at Mass (*S. C. R.*), or when a newly-ordained Priest says his first Mass.—*S. C. R.* In Rome it is customary for the parish Priests to wear the stole when preaching; any Priest will do so when preaching in presence of the Bishop.—*S. C. R., Nov.* 12, 1831. The Fathers of any Regular Order do not wear the stole, as they preach vested in their religious habit.—*S. C. R.*.

10. *Maniple*, to have three crosses like the stole, and ribbons with which to fasten it securely to the arm.—*Gav.* It should be about 3 feet 4 inches long, from end to end, inclusive of the fringe, which is like that on the stole.

The Maniple is worn with the chasuble, only when celebrating Mass, and at part of the ceremonial of Good Friday, but never with the cope.—*Rubr. Miss.*

11. *Cope*, of semicircular form, about 4 feet 10 inches long, so as to reach below the ankles. The border in front from top to bottom is ornamented with gold or silk embroidery, as also the hood behind; the fringe of the latter will be wider than that round the bottom.—*Gav.* The cope is fastened in front with a clasp or *morse*, and two or three large hooks.—*Gav.* It should never be fastened with strings so as to bring the hood (or border above it) close down upon the neck. The copes used in Rome by the Cope-men at Vespers are of a plainer description, having the border in front merely marked out by stripes of lace, and the hood plain, without a centre ornament.

12. *Dalmatic*, the sacred vestment of the Deacon, should not have mere lappets upon the shoulders, but wide sleeves reaching to the hands. The length of the dalmatic is rather more than 3½ feet, the width at the shoulders 21 inches, the circumference at the bottom 5 feet 9 inches. From the fastening on each shoulder there may be clusters of large tassels, hanging down before and behind. The circumference of the sleeves, at the jointure 31½ inches, at the hands 25½ inches.

13. *Tunic* for the Subdeacon, like the dalmatic of the Deacon, except that the sleeves are narrower and somewhat shorter.—*Cær. Ep.* In Rome, from long custom, they are of the same size as the dalmatic.

14. *Humeral Veil*, to be about 7 feet 10 inches long, exclusive of the fringe, and about 3 feet wide; the fringe at both ends should be similar to that on the stole and maniple: some sacred emblem may be worked in gold or silk embroidery in the centre. This veil should be of the same material as the set of vestments to which it belongs, and be lined with plain silk.

15. *Veil of the Chalice*, to be about 24 inches square, and to be ornamented all round with a narrow border of silk, gold, or silver; to be lined with plain silk. No cross or emblem is prescribed to be worked upon the centre; in Rome they are most commonly without it.

16. *Burse*, to have a Cross or other sacred emblem worked on the centre of the front (*Gav.*); mere quatrefoils and trefoils can scarcely be thought sufficient. The back to be plain but of the same material as the front; to be lined with white silk or linen. Those used at Rome are about 10½ inches square and have the front bordered round with lace the same as on the vestments; the Cross in the centre is also of the same lace. On each of the corners of the burse used at Rome is fastened a small tassel without fringe, in size and form not unlike a small acorn. These are useful, as they prevent the burse from slipping when placed against the back of the Altar.

17. *Veil of the Ciborium*, to be of white silk or cloth of gold (*Conc. West.*), drawn together at the top, but having an opening to allow the Cross which surmounts the cover to pass through.

18. *Antependium*, to be a little longer than the Altar, and to reach to the predella. At a distance of about 8 inches from the top to be ornamented with fringe more or less rich, according to its quality. It may have a Cross, an image of the Saint to whom the Altar is dedicated, or some other sacred emblem worked in the centre. Pope Zachary offered one of cloth of gold, with an image of our Lord, to the Altar of St. Peter. If possible the antependium should be fastened to a frame of wood, having the inner edges chamfered off, lest the material of the veil be injured. If the veil be costly, a covering may be neatly put over it, yet only in time of Mass, lest the Priest be impeded, or his vest-

ments injured : this covering should not extend below the fringe.—*Gav.*

There seems little reason why the embroidery should be so much *in relievo* as to require the covering Gavantus speaks of.

The antependia now generally used in Rome are of plain (yet in many instances very rich) material; they have no centre ornament but the deep fringe, about 8 or 10 inches from the top, which runs horizontally from end to end. The veil below the fringe is marked out into compartments by perpendicular strips of lace of silk, gold, or silver, according to the colour and richness of the material. Between the top and the horizontal fringe there are smaller compartments formed also by perpendicular strips of lace which intersect those below the fringe, in the following form, the double line of which is supposed to represent the deep fringe :—

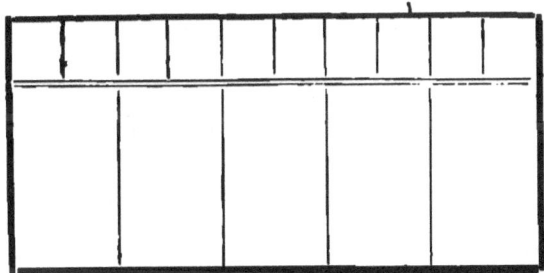

The frame is defined by a gilt border, that running along the bottom being wider than the rest.[1]

It is recommended to have transparent covers of glazed gauze to be used out of the times of Divine offices, when a costly antependium cannot be replaced by one of ordinary material. It is also recommended to have an extra white antependium, not fixed upon a frame, but by hooks or other means, made so that it may be fastened to the upper

---

[1] The author has drawn the frontispiece of the 2nd and two subsequent editions of the *Ceremonial according to the Roman Rite*, especially to show how well a Roman Antependium is suited to an Altar built and decorated in the Gothic manner.

part of the frames of others. It would be used for Benediction of the Most Holy Sacrament, under circumstances
when the antependium has to be changed whilst the congregation are assembled; as for instance when Vespers having
been sung in Red, are to be followed by the Benediction.[1]
The unsightly carrying about of frames would be thus
avoided. The black antependia should not be ornamented
with figures emblematical of death.—*S. C. R.*

19. *Veil of the Tabernacle,* to be made of rich material,
white or other colour, according to the feast; to be
gathered in full at the top, and to be sufficiently ample to
cover the whole of the Tabernacle; to be bordered around
with fringe.—*Gav.* When the ornaments of the Altar are
black, this veil will be purple.—*Baldeschi and others.*

20. *Alb* should be of linen, 6 feet long, and about 12
feet in circumference at the bottom; the sleeves 27 inches
long, and $17\frac{1}{2}$ inches wide at the shoulders, but narrowing
gradually to the hands.—*Gav.* In Italy they are more or
less ornamented with lace from the waist downwards. The
Congregation of Rites has forbidden a transparent material
lined with red to be used at the bottom, or on the sleeves.[2]
Because apparelled albs have squares of coloured material
outside, they are not thought to be included in this decree;
at least, they are unrecognized by any authors on the present Roman Rite.

21. *Amice,* to be of fine linen, about 31 inches square;
the two front corners to have strings. It should have a
Cross worked with the needle, in the middle, at two fingers'
width from the upper part. The borders, except that one
which surrounds the neck, may be ornamented with plain
work.—*Gav.* Apparelled amices are not known as a Roman
vestment.

22. *Girdle* should not be of silk, but of linen (*S. C. R.*);
Gavantus says of white flax or thin hemp, about $10\frac{1}{2}$ feet

---

[1] It is only at times when the Officiant leaves the Sanctuary, between
Vespers and Benediction, that the antependium is to be changed.—See the
Ritus Servandus.

[2] An liceat ubique terrarum in fimbriis et manicis albarum, et aliarum
vestium, sub velo transparenti, fundum rubrum mittere, vel an sit privi-
legium peculiare Italiæ, Hispaniæ? Resp. *negative.*—*Die* 17 Aug., 1833.

long, the ends inserted into tassels of the same material. It is allowed to be of the colour of the vestments (*S. C. R.*); but white is used at Rome, and is generally preferred by Rubricians.

23. *Cotta*—its form is that of a T, and does not exceed 24 inches (exclusive of lace one inch wide) in length, for one of middle size. The sleeves are 17 inches long (exclusive of lace), and 32 inches in circumference; the shoulder-pieces about 4½ inches square, edged with narrow lace; the circumference of the body 8 feet 8 inches. Although the mediæval surplice does not strictly come within the terms of the decree of the Council of Westminster (*Decree* xviii. n. 1), which says that the form of the *sacred* ornaments is to be assimilated to those in use at Rome; yet it cannot be doubted but that the *spirit* of the decree is, that this, as well as other vestments, also should be of the Roman pattern. Surplices without sleeve, or with wings sewn on behind, are not known in Rome.

24. *Rochet*, like the cotta, except that the sleeves are rather tight, tapering down to the hand like those of the albs. The rochet is worn by Canons, but only under the mozetta. When administering baptism, or other sacraments, they do not wear it, but the ordinary cotta. A Canon's rochet is less ornamented with lace and borders than that of a Bishop, and, unless by special privilege, should not have red material showing from beneath at the wrists.—*Gav.*

25. *Corporal*, to be of fine white linen, about 19½ inches square, with an additional border of thread lace 1⅜ inches wide. To be folded in four, so that no border appear outside. In the fore part, that is, in the centre of one of the squares made by the folds, a Cross should be worked in white. The above are those generally used at Rome. Suarez says they may have a light border of silk and gold.

The corporal is blessed together with the pall (*Pont. Rom.*), and, after use, may not be touched by Laics, unless with especial permission, nor washed after use in domestic vessels (*Ord. Rom.*), until they have been first washed by a Clerk in Holy Orders, when they may be touched by Laics until again used.—*Sylv.* v. Those corporals which have been employed at the Altar should be left in the Burses, and not be taken out and put away in drawers.

26. *Pall.*—Those at present used at Rome are about 4½ inches square, with a border of linen thread lace 1⅜ inches wide; it is made of stout linen, doubled, but having no card placed between, and has a white Cross worked in the centre. When made up by the laundress, they should be made as stiff as possible with starch to which some white wax has been added. Palls having the upper side of silk are prohibited by the Sacred Congregation of Rites.

27. *Purificator,* to be of linen, neither coarse nor fine, to be simply hemmed, and not less than 13½ inches square, with a very small Cross worked in the centre.—*Gav.* Although it is not required to be blessed, yet, when once employed in the Sacrifice of the Mass, it should not be used for other purposes, nor be handled by Laics (not having the requisite permission), until after having been washed by a Clerk in Holy Orders. The same rules for washing purificators are to be observed as for corporals. (See n. 25 above.)

28. *Napkins,* or towels for the fingers, to be of linen, 36 inches long and 27 wide; the edges may have fringe or narrow lace of the same material.—*Gav.*

29. *Altar Cloths.*—Every Altar is required to be covered with three linen cloths, in addition to that which is waxed, and which covers the consecrated stone. The under ones should not exceed the length of the table of the Altar; but the uppermost one should hang down at each end to the top step, and will be rather wider than the table of the Altar. It may have five crosses worked on it, one in the centre, and one at each angle. Altar cloths having borderings of various colours and patterns, with monograms, &c., are not used at Rome.

30. *Communion Cloths,* to be of linen, 3 feet wide, and of various lengths, to suit the rails to which they are to be attached.

31. *Altar Cover* should be of green colour (*Cær. Ep.*), and in size rather more than to cover the table of the altar; it should have a border of narrow fringe.—*Gav.* Cloth or fine baize is recommended.

32. *Credence Cloths*, to be of white linen, and of such sizes that each credence may be covered, either so that the cloth reach on all sides down to the ground, or but a short distance over the surface of the table.

33. *Seat Covers*, some to be of green, others of purple; one of each, about 4½ yards long, for the seat of the Sacred Ministers at solemn Mass; others square, for the stools which are used on various occasions.

34. *Lectern Hangings*, of the various colours, and of materials more or less costly. The size, of course, to be determined by the lecterns.

35. *Altar Cushions* for the Missal, of various colours and richness; they should not be filled with feathers, but with wool or deer's hair. To be about 18 inches long and 13½ wide, sewn plainly, but ornamented with tassels at the corners.—*Gav.* In some churches, altar-desks or book-stands are considered more convenient; the latter may be furnished with veils of the usual colours, which should be a little wider than the desk, and sufficiently long that they may hang about four inches over the top, and about the same below the ledge upon which the book rests. The veil may have a border of lace braid about 1 inch wide, and the lower be ornamented with gold or silk fringe about 2 inches deep.

36. *Veil of Exposition*, to be of white costly material, embroidered with gold and silver; about 3 feet square; to hang banner-wise from an ornamented stand, sufficiently high, when placed on the Altar, to screen from view the Most Holy Sacrament exposed on the Throne. It is used during sermons given at the time of solemn Exposition.

37. *The Sacred Vessels* are the chalice, paten, monstrance, ciborium, and pyx for the Communion of the Sick, none of which may be handled by those not in Holy Orders, unless with especial permission.—*S. C. R.*

The stocks containing the Holy oils are also, in a certain sense, called Sacred vessels, although they have not received a particular benediction.

38. *The Chalice and Paten* are consecrated by the Bishop with the Holy Chrism. Either will lose this consecration when it is broken or otherwise damaged; it will also re-

quire to be consecrated anew after having been re-gilt.—
S. C. R., June 14, 1845. When repairs are needed, application should be made to the Bishop, who will declare them
unfit for use ; they may then be handled by the workmen.

The chalice should have a boss or knob, about the
middle of the stem, not so ornamented as to be inconvenient when taken in the hand, while the thumb and fore-
finger are joined. The cup, at least, is to be of silver, gilt
within (*Conc. West.*); its circumference, at the brim, not
less than 10½ inches, and the height of the chalice not less
than 9 inches.—*Gav.* The paten should be of gold or
silver, gilt on the surface of the upper side ; the rim thin
enough to be of use in collecting the Sacred Particles, and
not less than 24 inches in circumference.

39. *The Monstrance* should be of material as costly as
can be well afforded ; the *lunette*, that part in which the
Most Holy Sacrament is placed, should be of gold or silver
gilt ; it is placed in the centre of a circle of rays resembling
a sun.—*Cær. Ep. ; Bar.* tit. 80, n. 31.

The monstrance was formerly of a cylindrical form ;
those, however, now used at Rome are as described, surrounded by rays, and surmounted by a small Cross without a figure of our Lord. The monstrance of cylindrical
pattern may be readily and artistically brought within the
precincts of the Rubrics by the addition of rays in form of
an oval nimbus.

40. *Ciborium.*—The cup to be at least of silver, gilt
within ; the stem like that of the chalice, but shorter ; the
bottom of the inside should be a little elevated, so that
the Sacred Particles, when few in number, may be easily
taken up ; the cover to be surmounted with a very small
Cross.

41. *Pyx*, for the Communion of the Sick, should have its
case or cover of rich white silk, and, even when empty, may
be kept in the Tabernacle, in which the Most Holy Sacrament reposes.—*Gardellini and others.*

42. *Holy Oil Stocks.*—The oil stock for the sick should
have a case of purple silk (*Bar.*); it should be preserved
in the ambry, on the Gospel side of the High Altar,
or, if there be not one, in some convenient place in the

Sacristy, or Presbytery (*Conc. West.*, decr. xx. n. 4), but never in the Tabernacle on the Altar.—*S. C. ·R.* The Sacred Congregation of Rites allows it to be preserved in the house of the Priest who resides at a distance from the Church, even when there is a proper ambry for it.—*14th May*, 1826. The Council of Westminster has not determined anything under such circumstances.

The Holy Chrism and oil of catechumens are to be preserved in the ambry of the Baptistery, or, where there is not one, in the Sacristy.—*Conc. West.*

43. *Cruets*, not to be of silver or other metal, but of glass or crystal and to have suitable stoppers.—*Gav.* Although these are almost universally used in Rome, yet those of metal are sometimes seen.· When of metal, that for the water has the letter A (*aqua*) on the cover; and that for the wine, V (*vinum*). The glass ones are recommended, provided they have tubular spouts, like those used at Rome, which have several advantages over those of metal.

After use, the cruets, especially those of metal, should be rinsed out, and placed upside down in a frame or rack, that they may drain. To absorb the drops which fall, let a square piece of *spongio piline* be placed underneath : it may be procured at the chemist's.

44. *Cruet Stand* to be of the same material as the cruets, —roomy, and flat within ; to be ornamented, but not so as to prevent the cruets standing safely on it. This stand is used for the washing of the Priest's fingers during Mass; another is not required. The Bishop, as also the Priest on some rare occasions, uses an ewer and basin.

45. *Spoon;* its use for putting water into the chalice is not sanctioned by the Sacred Congregation of Rites (7th September, 1850) ; nor is it required where cruets with spouts are used. It is very well to have one ready at hand in the Sacristy, should, for instance, a fly get into the chalice during the Canon ; but such is of rare occurrence.

46. *Liturgical Books* should be kept in a press or cupboard by themselves ; the larger ones, such as Missals, each in a separate compartment. The covers are often injured by rubbing against others, especially if ornamented with metal-work. The more costly books may each have a case

of saffron-dyed baize, made so as to button over at one end. It injures the Missals to leave the markers in them, especially when twisted.

The Missal is sometimes covered for Mass; this cover should be made of silk velvet or other rich material, suitably embroidered with gold or silver; it should not project at the top, but may fall about five inches below the book. The edges of the cover may be bound with silk, and that of the lower part have a narrow fringe. They are made to fasten by means of small buttons and silk tapes on the inner side of the cover of the Missal. A number of these covers may be obtained to suit the various colours of the Church. Those of black for Masses for the dead, should be plainer, and not have ornaments emblematical of death worked upon them.

The Sacristan should be well acquainted with the names and number of the books intrusted to his care; he should know the occasions when they are respectively required, and have them in readiness for any emergency.

The following is a list of books with which the Sacristy should be furnished :—

1. *Missale Romanum*, for Mass.

2. *Supplementum Miss.* for Masses of Saints proper to England, Ireland and Scotland.

3. *Liber Epistolarum*, for the Deacon and Subdeacon at high Mass.

4. *Graduale Romanum.*

5. *Ritus Servandus*, for the Benediction of the Most Holy Sacrament, the Asperges, and some other occasions.

6. *Vesperale Romanum*, for Vespers.

7. *Processionale Romanum*, for the Asperges and Processions.[1]

8. *Rituale Romanum*, for the administration of Holy Baptism, Extreme Unction, and Matrimony; also for the Churching of Women, the Blessing of Water,

9. *Liber Status Animarum.*

10. *Liber Baptizatorum*, for the registration of Baptisms.[1]

11. *Liber Confirmatorum*, for the registration of Confirmations.

12. *Liber Defunctorum*, for the registration of Burials.

13. *Liber Matrimoniorum*, for the registration of Marriages.

It is recommended that each Sacristy should be furnished with one or more copies of some authorized manual of ceremonies, which may be consulted at any time by those employed in the Divine offices.

47. *Tables of Prayers*, before and after Mass, framed and glazed, or, which is preferable, neatly mounted on stout cardboard, edged with leather and varnished, should be hung against the wall directly in front of the *prie-dieu* or kneeling-desk, where the Priest may make preparation and thanksgiving before and after Mass. In Rome, small books containing these prayers are fastened by small chains to the various kneeling-desks.

48. *Tables of Rules for the Sacristies* should be suitably mounted, and hung up in convenient places. The *formulæ* given in Appendix I. as specimens, may be altered or modified, according to local circumstances, by the Priest of the mission. There are but few congregations in which some person may not be found who would consider it a pleasurable task to copy out such documents in a becoming style ; or they may be printed at a very small expense.

49. *Silence Board.*—Every Sacristy should have hung up, in a conspicuous place, a board on which the word " Silence " is painted in large and unmistakable characters. The Sacristan, by his example, will encourage others to observe that religious tone which should always pervade the Sacristy. It may, at first, cost him some little trouble, yet, after a short perseverance, he will have formed a habit of never conversing on worldly subjects, and of never diverging from

---

[1] The books for registration of marriages, baptisms, and burials, are of course not required in every church.

an undertone when speaking of matters necesssary to the discharge of his duties.

50. *The Thurible, Incense-boat, Spoon, and Canister of Incense* should be kept together in a cupboard. It is recommended to let the thuribles hang from pegs, and the other articles stand upon a shelf a little above. The incense commonly used at Rome is simple *Gum Olibanum*, and may be obtained from the wholesale chemist, and at a moderate price. 2 oz. of Gum Benzoin, and 1 oz. of powdered Cascarilla Bark, added to each pound of Gum Olibanum, will be found an agreeable compound.

51. *Fire for the Thurible.*—Where gas is laid on in the Sacristy, it will be found both convenient and economical to have a jet fitted with a frame, upon which may rest a small iron pan, so perforated that the charcoal put into it may easily be ignited by the flame of the gas passing through. The pan should have a small handle. This plan is especially useful in the summer season, as, by a gutta-percha tubing, the jet may be temporarily placed in the ordinary stove or fire-place; and during the winter months, when the coal fires are burning, may be carefully laid by. If the jet used is that of a "Bunsen's Burner," the charcoal will be ignited in about two minutes. For heating charcoal in the ordinary fire, a bowl made of iron wire, with a handle, is both useful and economical.

52. *The Holy Water Vessel* should be emptied and wiped out immediately after use. It is recommended to have also an earthen vessel with a cover in which to preserve the Holy Water, and from which the vessels and stoups of the Church may be supplied.

53. *The Aspersory* should be wiped dry after use, and carefully laid by, but always together with the Holy Water vessel.

54. *Acolytes' Candlesticks*, to have a round, or, which would be better, a triangular base: they should be smaller than those of the High Altar.—*Gav.* It is a common fault to have them too small; unless of tolerable size, they look unsightly when placed on the floor of the Sanctuary during Vespers. They should have a boss or knob at the middle of the stem.

55. *Torches.*—Those used in Rome are formed of four large wax candles ; such, however, are unsuited to England, as our Sanctuaries are generally carpeted, and the wax is apt to drop. Very suitable torches may be made of wood, grooved to resemble four candles, *i.e.*, the section of which would be a quatrefoil. These may be painted white, and hollowed out to receive a large-sized Palmer's candle-spring. They should have a hollow at the top, to retain any wax that might gutter. In these torches, the ends of the larger candles from the Altar candlesticks might be used up. Let the socket of the spring have a small aperture near the top, so that, without taking out the candle, it may be seen whether there is sufficient for the occasion required. The ends of larger candles are recommended for this purpose, as the flame of a torch should naturally be larger than that of an ordinary candle; for this reason also, the author does not recommend those brass standards in which mere tapers are placed, as in candlesticks. Eight torches may be used on the great festivals. They should be kept in a rack, which is either in a cupboard, or at least capable of being covered over.

56. *Processional Cross,* to be made to take off the staff, as, at the burial of an infant, it is carried without it (*Rit. Rom.*) ; it should have its cover, to prevent damage from dust. Processional Crosses having images of the Blessed Virgin and Saint John, added on brackets, are never used at Rome.

57. *Processional Banners* should not be of triangular form, nor resemble those used for military purposes (*Bar.*) ; the staff should be surmounted by a small Cross.—*Ibid.* Banners are employed to excite the devotion of the Faithful, especially of the poor, for whose sakes, therefore, the emblems and mottoes worked on them should be such as they can readily understand. When not in use, the banners should be detached from the staves, and each carefully put away ; when left about, they are very liable to be thrown down and damaged. This remark applies also to the processional Cross, verger's staff, &c.

58. *Verger's Staff,* the use of which is recognized in the Ceremonial of Bishops (Book 2, chap xxvii. n. 5), is usually

surmounted by an emblem of the Patron Saint of the Church,
or some other appropriate design.

59. *Processional Lanterns*, fixed on the top of high staves,
should be made to contain candles, and not oil-lamps. They
are used at funeral and other processions which pass into the
open air. They should have covers put on them when not
in use, as they are very apt to tarnish if not kept with
especial care.

60. *Processional Canopies* or *Baldacchini* are of three kinds.
The *first* is that of white costly material, which is supported
by six or eight staves (*Cær. Ep.*), and which is carried over
the Most Holy Sacrament in solemn procession. It should
be ornamented around with double hangings nine inches
wide, with deep fringe inside and outside.—*Gav.* Small
bells hanging from the borders are not used in Rome, nor
are the staves usually surmounted with small Crosses. The
second is that of less costly material, and may vary in colour
according to the feast. It is carried over the Bishop, and, like
the former, may have six or eight staves.—*Cær. Ep.*, lib. i.
cap. xiv. n. 1. The *third* is the small canopy or *ombrella*,
which is used for the removal of the Blessed Sacrament
within the Church, and to the homes of the sick in localities
where it is customary. This canopy may be deeply fringed
around, and the ribs of it be made to open flat, so that it
may resemble as little as possible one of ordinary use. It
will of course be white.

61. *Processional Images* should be preserved with the
greatest care: if exposed on brackets in the Church or
Sacristy, they should be carefully dusted from time to time.
There should be some means by which the image may be
fastened to the bier upon which it is carried: the neglect of
this precaution has often been regretted after some un-
pleasant accident. The bier should not be decorated in a
tawdry manner, but with simplicity and good taste. Care
should also be taken in the arrangement of any draperies
which may clothe the image. Nothing can be more un-
meaning and unnatural than draperies edged round with
large wreaths of flowers—often artificial ones, not of very
recent manufacture. Let flowers only be employed in places

and positions in which they might naturally be looked for—in vases and the like.

62. *Paschal Candlestick*, used from Holy Saturday to the morning of the Ascension inclusively. It should, at other times, have its cover, and be laid up in a convenient place; care should also be taken of the candle (which is again required for the Blessing of the Font on the Vigil of Pentecost), and of the grains of incense, if enclosed in ornamental cases. The whole should be suitably covered.

63. The *Triangular Candlestick*, for the *Tenebræ Offices* of Holy Week, should have its cover, and be laid by in a convenient place. It is recommended that articles of this kind should be looked to about once a month. Accumulated *dust* may be removed, but accumulated *rust* is almost unremovable. The Sacristan of short memory may conveniently appoint for himself a particular time for the fulfilment of such duties—say the first Monday of each month.

64. *Triple-branched Reed*, for Holy Saturday, to be also carefully laid by as the above.

65. *Lecterns*, portable and of convenient height. Those commonly used in Rome consist of two frames of gilt metal or polished wood, so fastened by bolts as to open in the form of an X. The arms of one frame are longer than those of the other, so that the stout leather which connects the upper part of the frames should form an incline upon which the book may rest. On festive occasions these. Lecterns are covered with hangings or veils of the appropriate colour. They should be as wide as the leather, about 6 feet long, and be trimmed with a neat border of lace braid, with the addition of fringe at the two ends. In large churches three lecterns are required for Holy Week. The more substantial lecterns of the choir of singers are not covered with veils.

66. *Flower Vases* should be carefully wiped out after use, especially those of metal. General rules on their use are given elsewhere; it is, however, as well here to remark, that the circumstance of their not being wanted in the Sanctuaries of the Church is no reason why they should be

displayed to adorn the Sacristy. Let them, therefore, be put away in a cupboard, and, unless wanted again within a very short time, let the flowers (if natural) be taken out. Artificial flowers should have a drawer entirely appropriated to them.

67. *Bells.*—There should be a bell, large enough to be heard throughout the Church, hung just without the Sacristy door, the string of which may be conveniently pulled as one enters the Church. If a hand-bell, it may be placed on a bracket near the door. This bell is rung by the Server when the Priest leaves the Sacristy to say a Low Mass, and not at other times. When there are two Sacristies, there may be a communication from near the large vesting press to a bell in the outer Sacristy. The Master of Ceremonies rings it when the Sacred Ministers commence to vest, in order that those in the outer Sacristy may be warned to put themselves into processional order.

68. *Lavatory,* to be well supplied with pure water, and to have a tap and basin, with a pipe to carry off the waste water. A towel should hang on one side, near at hand. On no account should the Sacristan wash his hands there, or allow others employed about the Sacristies to do so. For such there should be water, soap, and towels, in some retired place without the Sacristy. The cruets may be rinsed out at the lavatory. The practice of stopping up the pipe, and allowing water to stand in the basin for the purpose of putting flowers in it, should be avoided.

69. *Kneeling-desk* or *Prie-Dieu,* to be suitably covered with green baize, and be placed in a retired part of the inner Sacristy. The tables of prayers for before and after Mass, should hang immediately in front of it.

70. *Bread Canisters.*—That for the large breads to be of such a size that the breads may be easily taken out, and to have a round piece of sheet-lead, covered with linen or silk, to keep them flat. Some few of each sort of breads should be kept ready cut, in case they should be wanted at a short notice.

71. *Cassocks* and *Birrettas* should be kept in readiness, if it is likely that Priests will visit the Church and require them.

The cassock should descend at least to the heels : *saltem talum pedis attingat.* The word *saltem* supposes it may descend a little lower, perhaps to the ground. A Priest, Archdeacon, Archpriest, or even the Vicar-General, if not a Protonotary Apostolic or Prelate of the Roman Court, has not the right to a cassock with the train, which supposes the services of a train-bearer (*S. C. R.* 17th June, 1673 ; *Fornici* and others). In Rome, the Parish Priests are distinguished from their Curates by wearing a broad silk girdle over their cassock. The addition of a cape and double sleeves to the simple cassock is properly an indication of superiority among the clergy. A slight confusion may possibly exist in some instances between the *zimarra*, spoken of the first Provincial Synod of Westminster (page 77), and a cassock with these additions. The *zimarra* is properly a domestic garment worn over the cassock (supra vestem, vulgo *zimarra.* Bened. XIII., Method S. Visitat.), and is not uncommonly furnished with a cape even in the case of simple ecclesiastics.

72. The *Candles* should be kept in drawers by themselves, and the greatest care taken of the ends and refuse wax, which may be sent to the chandler to be again melted down. The Sacred Congregation has decided that candles of sperm, composition, or other substance, may not be used on the Altar in lieu of wax (16th Sept., 1843). Large quantities of *animal* stearine are made up into "Church candles," and sold as "*vegetable* wax." Oil lamps may be used in extreme scarcity (*S. C. R.*). Painted Altar candles are a prerogative of the Sovereign Pontiff.

The wicks of candles should always be looked to before they are lighted, and generally the tops cut off smooth, so that they are not too long and have no excrescences at the top, otherwise they are liable to gutter and waste the wax ; the wicks of candles for benediction may be touched with *Venice* turpentine—a very *minute* particle—that they may be more easily lighted when the function is about to commence.

73. *Charcoal*, to be kept in a covered vase. To prevent damage by dust, and inconvenience at the moment it is required for use, let it be broken into proper sizes before

it is brought into the Sacristy. The small tongs should be kept with it in the vase.

1. The *High Altar* may be 3 feet 6 inches high, or at most 3 feet 7½ inches; and 7½ feet long, or longer, if in a large church, and at least 3 feet 9 inches wide.—*Gav.* The above measurement includes the space occupied by the steps for the Cross and candlesticks.

It is strictly prohibited to use the underneath part of the Altar as a cupboard, or recess to put things in.—*S. C. R.*

There may be one or more steps upon the High Altar, but space should if possible be left to walk round it. The candlesticks on the steps should not seem to be off the Altar, on account of the Rubrics for the incensation.—*Gav.* The size of the step on a side-Altar given by Gavantus, is 6 inches wide and as many deep; it would be proper to have it proportionally larger according to the relative size of the Altar. For the antependium, see No. 18, page 7.

2. *The Steps to the Altar and the Pavement.*—There should be three steps, including the predella as one.—*Corsetti and others.* The predella should be 6 inches longer at each end than the Altar; and 3 feet wide, that is, from the front of the Altar. Each step should be 6 inches high. —*Gav.* The space between the lowest step and the rails of the sanctuary should be 12 feet, or, in some churches not collegiate, 6 feet.—*Gav.* By "collegiate" is understood those churches which have stalls in the choir or Sanctuary, where the Divine office is publicly recited.

The remainder of the sanctuary should be a plane, and not be subdivided into a number of platforms. The plane for which the term pavement is used, should be covered with green carpeting (*Cær. Ep.*) up to the base of the steps. The steps and predella may be covered with more costly material, variously ornamented according to the season.— *Cær. Ep.* The carpeting should be fastened down in such a manner that it may be easily removed when occasion requires; such as at Masses for the Dead, and the offices of Holy Week. It is recommended that the carpet should cover the full extent of the Sanctuary. In this particular the practice of southern climates cannot be advisably adopted in England, at least in the winter season. Encaustic tiles are often found exceedingly inconvenient. Priests, when carrying the Sacred vessels, have always more or less anxiety lest they should lose their footing. Boys and young persons are especially liable to unwary accidents. It is recommended that the tiles should be covered, particularly those parts over which the clergy and attendants walk.

Floors which are at all damp injure the carpets very much. If the dampness cannot be prevented, the carpets should, if possible, not be left down. In such cases it is economical to place cocoa-nut matting underneath; this may also be adopted on stone floors in cold churches. Crosses are not to be sculptured upon the pavement (*Manuale Ep.*), nor (by a parity of reason) be depicted on tiles, nor wrought in the carpets.

The steps to the Episcopal throne are spoken of at No. 20 below.

3. The *Tabernacle* is prescribed to be of wood by the Fourth Provincial Council of Milan, and by the Council of Bishops; it is also generally spoken of as such by all liturgical writers. In a country where there is danger of sacrilege, it is desirable to have a case of iron within, which may again be lined with boards of poplar-wood to prevent damp, which Gavantus recommends. By a decree of the Council of Bishops (October 25th, 1575), the exterior of the Tabernacle is to be gilt, and the interior lined throughout with white silk. The door should have on it some Sacred emblem—the most usual are a Chalice and Host, or a figure of Christ rising from the Tomb.—*Castald.* The key, which should be gilt, is to be committed to the care of the Priest.—*Conc. West.*

The Tabernacle should stand back not less than 2 feet 6 inches from the front of the Altar, so that the corporal may be fully extended.—*Gav.*

The Tabernacle is exclusively reserved for the preservation of the Most Holy Sacrament. The vessels containing the Sacred Species are to be covered each with a white veil (see No. 17, page 6), and to rest upon a clean corporal spread within the Tabernacle. The Sacred Congregation of Rites forbids Relics of the Passion, or of the Saints, or the Holy Oils, to be placed within the Tabernacle. Cavalieri says that the Sacred vessels, even when they do not contain the Most Holy Sacrament, may be left within, since they appertain directly to It; but Baruffaldi maintains the contrary. The Tabernacle, at times when it contains the Most Holy Sacrament, *and then only,* should be covered with its veil of the colour of the day (see No. 19, page 8). This veil is put on or exchanged at the same time as the antependium.

4. The *Throne for Exposition* is not necessarily to be connected with the Tabernacle; according to the opinion of many, it is better separate. Where the Altar is large, and removed some distance from the wall, the throne may be approached by permanent steps behind the Altar; but when the Altar is small, and near the wall, it may be placed on ornamental brackets against the wall, and be approached from the front. It should on no account be so placed that the Cross cannot stand between the Candlesticks (*S. C. R.; Cær. Ep.; Gav.,* and others), or that a seventh candle cannot be placed behind the Cross when the Bishop celebrates. —*Cær. Ep.* The throne is required to have a canopy or covering above (*S. C. R.*); a mere metal crown, the interior of which is not filled in, is insufficient.

5. The *Cross* is supposed, by the Ceremonial of Bishops, to have a figure of our Lord, to be of the same material as the Candlesticks, and so high that the foot of the Cross may be level with the top of the candlesticks (Book 1, chap. 12, n. 11). In Rome, the base and stem of the Cross are usually of the same pattern as those of the candlesticks. According to the Constitution of Benedict XIV., July 16th, 1746, the Cross is to be placed between the candlesticks; the image of Christ Crucified to be of such dimensions as to be readily seen both by the Celebrant and people. The question has been put to the Sacred Congregation of Rites, whether a small Crucifix, placed upon the Tabernacle, or upon a stand in the centre of the Altar, will satisfy the Rubric, which requires one to be placed between the

candlesticks? The answer pronounced it an abuse to be reprobated, and declared that if, on account of any accidental cause, the Cross was required to be removed from between the candlesticks, another smaller might be used during the Holy Sacrifice, yet this one must be visible as well to the people as to the Priest (17th September, 1832). The Sacred Congregation has also decreed, that where there is a large statue of the Crucifix at the Altar, a second one upon it is not required (16th June, 1663); and Benedict XIV., in the Constitution *Accepimus*, has decided that there is no need of a Cross on the Altar where there is a large painting in which our Lord upon the Cross is the most prominent part of the subject.

6. The *Candlesticks* should be six in number—three each side of the Cross; strictly speaking they are not to be of equal height, but to rise gradually towards the Cross.—*Cær. Ep.* The candlesticks should be furnished with white wax candles, except on some few occasions, which are mentioned elsewhere. When Low Masses are said at the High Altar, it is usual to have two smaller candlesticks on the lowest step. It is recommended that these be taken away when not required; the same may be said of those used for Benediction. The time and trouble of removing them is less than is required for cleaning them, when left exposed in the Church.

7. The *Reliquaries* used at Rome are of metal, or carved wood, gilt, and in shape something like Monstrances, except that the centre cases, which contain the Relics, are each[1] surrounded by two palm branches and not rays.[1] Each reliquary is surmounted by a small Cross, without a figure of our Lord. The reliquaries are generally four in number, being placed between the candlesticks. Relics may be placed in the centre, but not upon or before the Tabernacle in which the Holy Sacrament reposes (*S. O. R.* 1845); they may in no case be placed on any part of the Altar, or on any table near it, when the Blessed Sacrament

---

[1] Specimens of Reliquaries, in Gothic pattern, may be seen in the frontispiece of the *Ceremonial according to the Roman Rite*. They are drawn from a sketch made by the author in the church of St. Vicenti, at Avila, in Spain.

is publicly exposed (*S. C. R.*); the time of Benediction, given either with the Monstrance or ciborium, would seem to be included.

The Altar should be adorned with reliquaries only on the more solemn occasions; there need not be additional candles lighted on that account, yet when left upon the Altar, four candles at least should be burning. —*S. C. R.*

8. *Statuettes* of the Saints, in gold or silver-gilt, are, in Rome, often placed upon the Altars during the great festivals. The Ceremonial of Bishops says they may be placed between the candlesticks, as the reliquaries. The same rules may be observed as with the reliquaries; that is, they should not be placed upon or before the Tabernacle when the Most Holy Sacrament reposes within it; nor should they be placed upon the Altar, or upon any table near the Altar, during Solemn Benediction or Exposition. —*S. C. R.* There seems no reason why a statuette may not be placed in the centre of an Altar at which the Holy Sacrament is not preserved. Baldeschi makes provision for such, in his remarks on the incensing of the Altar; for, according to the Sacred Congregation, such statuettes, even if they do not enclose Relics, are to be incensed just as the Relics, of which mention is made above (21st March, 1744). These statuettes are not necessarily those of full-length figures, but are often busts standing upon pedestals.

9. *Vases of Flowers* may be used as decorations for the Altar (*Cær. Ep.*); they should, however, be employed with taste and judgment, both as to quantity and quality. The things which should be most prominent on the Altar are its *furniture*, such as, for instance, the candlesticks. Mere *ornament* should never be employed in such quantities as to hide the furniture out of sight. This is one of the subjects on which the Sacristan should endeavour to form a correct taste. Remarks have been made elsewhere on the unmeaningness of putting flowers in places where they would seem unnatural, as, for instance, on borders of drapery, &c. (see page 19).

It is not allowed to place vases of flowers before the door

of the Tabernacle, upon which there is a representation of our Lord.—*S. C. R.* When natural flowers are employed, care should be taken not to allow the leaves to come in contact with the metal or gilt-work of candlesticks, reliquaries, &c., as the damp or vapour which passes off is apt to injure them. The vases should be of uniform shape and material. It has the appearance of very bad taste to see a number of odd vases crowded on the Altar, some of which are perhaps no better than those usually found in the dwellings of the most humble classes.

10. The *Altar Cloths*, as described at page 10, should *all* be kept clean, and not merely the uppermost one. The wax-cloth, which covers the consecrated stone, is not to be removed.

11. The *Altar Cover*, as at page 10, should be put on immediately after Mass, and left so during every other Divine Office or Function, except Benediction of the Most Holy Sacrament.

12. The *Antependium*, described at No. 18, page 7, should be placed or changed according to the colour of the feast. The following rule may be given : — Each afternoon the Sacristan should look at the *Ordo ;* and if the Vespers of the same day are marked down as V seq. (of the following day), or V a cap. seq. (from the chapter of the following day), he will determine that the colour *of the following day* should at once be used. If, however, the Vespers are the second of the present day, then the ornaments of the Altar should not be changed till after Vespers, or till the last thing at night or first thing in the morning, according to circumstances, provided it be done before Mass, or before Matins and Lauds, where sung. It is strongly recommended that this, and other things of the same kind, should be done at times when the Church is least frequented by the Faithful; and also that, as far as possible, all preparations should be made over-night—" Part of the work of to-day," says a good old proverb, " is to prepare for that of to-morrow."

13. The *Altar Cards* should not be left standing upon the Altar after the termination of the Masses ; nor should they be laid flat under the Altar-cover nor be left upon the

Credence, but be deposited in their proper place in the Sacristy.

14. The *Credence* should be about 4½ feet long, according to circumstances, or the size of the choir; 3 feet wide; and not higher than 3 feet 9 inches from the ground.—*Gav.* Care should be taken that it may be large enough to contain all required to be placed upon it for solemn functions. It is both inconvenient and unbecoming to have to place the Book of Epistles, &c., on the floor. In respect to the material and ornament, the Credence should be in keeping with the other furniture of the choir, as it ought not to be covered except for High Mass or other solemn functions.—*Corsetti.* The idea that a deal box, or anything else, will do well enough, so long as it is covered over, is obviously too irreverent to need further mention.

The proper place for the Credence is on the Epistle side (*Cær. Ep.*); it is recommended to place it, if possible, against the side-wall, and not against that where the Altar is. As a general rule, it should not be adorned with a Cross, flowers, or other ornaments; one only exception is given in the Ceremonial of Bishops, which allows large and costly vases of silver when a Cardinal celebrates, yet neither a Cross nor images of Saints (Book 1, chap. xii. n. 20).

15. The *Ambry for the Holy Oils* is a small Tabernacle fixed in the wall, near the Altar, *on the Gospel side of the Sanctuary.* The door should be of wood, have the words *Oleum Infirmorum* written legibly upon it, and be furnished with a lock and key.

This ambry, according to Baruffaldi, may be on the Gospel side of the Altar of the Holy Sacrament, so as to participate in the lights continually burning; but the Council of Westminister has enjoined that, in all churches to be built within that province, it shall be placed at the High Altar.

16. *Piscina,* a recess in the wall of the Sanctuary, on the Epistle side; it is fitted with a pipe to carry off the water poured into it, and usually has a shelf in the upper part, which, as St. Charles tells us, may be used for the cruets of wine and water at time of Mass. The piscina should be kept scrupulously clean, and on no account be used as a mere receptacle for candle-ends, dusters, &c.

17. The *Rails* should be fitted with hooks, to which the Communion cloths may be fastened. Every Altar in the Church should be railed in.—*Gav. and others.*

18. The *Communion Cloths* should be of the same length as the rails, to which they should be fastened before the Masses at which the faithful may present themselves for Holy Communion. When a habit of punctuality in this respect has been secured, the people will never be at a loss to know when and where they may present themselves, and much confusion will be avoided. Gavantus says that, after Mass, the Communion cloths should be taken away, and not be left exposed to the dust of the Church; the same is mentioned in the instructions of St. Charles to his clergy. The Communion cloths should be scrupulously clean, and never be allowed to fall to the ground. In folding them, after use, care should be taken not to allow them to sweep along the floor. Little improprieties of this kind shock the feelings of pious people and should by all means be avoided.

19. The *Seats for the Sacred Ministers* should be, in material and ornament, suitable to the rest of the furniture of the choir, as they are not covered, except when used, and not always then. That for the three Ministers during High Mass should be a form (*Cær. Ep.*), strictly speaking; in Rome it commonly has no back. It is about 7 feet long, and for the Mass (not at other times) is covered with a green baize, or, when the vestments are purple, with purple baize. At Masses for the Dead and on Good Friday it remains uncovered.

For Vespers, the Officiant, if he does not sit in the choir, will use a rather tall stool, covered with green or purple according to the season. The seats for the Cope-men and others are spoken of under the head of Preparations for the various Functions. When not required, the seats may be removed to where they are usually kept; in any case they should not be left here and there about the Sanctuary.

20. The *Episcopal Throne*, which is usually on the Gospel side of the Sanctuary, should be raised upon three steps, and be permanently fixed, only in the cathedral church;[1] it

---

[1] In collegiata nequit retineri sedes fixa pro Episcopo.—*S. R. C.* 26 Aprilis, 1834.

should have a canopy so constructed that it may be easily covered with ornamental hangings of the various colours appropriate to the Festivals of the Church.—*Cœrem. Epis.* The chair, with its high perpendicular back, may also be covered with the proper colour of the day; it should not be gilt, unless for a Cardinal.—*Cœr. Epis.* Square stools for the Assistant Priest and Deacons should be near the throne, and always be uncovered.—*Ibid.* In Italy, these latter are usually painted to resemble various marbles, the front displaying the Episcopal arms. The throne being fixed therefore only in the cathedral church, nothing appertaining to it should be allowed to remain in the Sanctuary of a parochial or collegiate church, except, of course, on the occasion of the visitation of a Bishop within his own diocese, or of a Cardinal or other high functionary. In this remark, the steps, which are considered as part of the throne, will be included.

21. *Lamps;* strictly, there should be hung before the High Altar three at least; or, if the Altar be that of the Blessed Sacrament, five at least.—*Cœr. Ep.* lib. i. cap. xii. n. 17. Although it is not customary in England to have lamps burning continually, unless before the Altar of the Blessed Sacrament; yet where a mission is well endowed, it would seem proper to have at least one burning before the High Altar, especially during the greater solemnities. The Sacred Congregation of Rites has prohibited lamps to be hung directly above any part of the table of the Altar. The lamps are not always made to hang; they may stand upon large candelabra, or upon brackets fixed against the side-walls. This latter method, although allowed for the lamps, is not so for the candles used for Mass (*S. C. R.*), which must be placed on the Altar. When the lamps hang from the ceiling, they should be made to move up and down by a double pulley. Step-ladders are unsightly objects to be brought before a congregation; for occasions will sometimes happen when it is necessary to do something to the lamps at the time the Faithful are assembled. Care is especially to be paid to the cords by which they are suspended. In churches where gas is burned, brass chains are unsafe, as they become rotten and break without any appa-

rent cause. Coloured cord, provided it be strong, and not liable to be chafed in the pulleys, is a better material.

The lamps are to be supplied with vegetable, not fish or animal, oil.—*S. C. R.* Before trimming the lamps, the Sacristan is recommended to lay a square piece of oilcloth or drugget on the floor beneath them. This precaution has often prevented considerable damage to the carpet when by accident the oil has been spilt.

22. The *Portable Steps*, for the Exposition, should be of sufficient height to enable the Priest easily to deposit the Monstrance upon the throne. At Rome, in some churches where the throne is high above the Altar, the upper portion of the steps is contrived so as to fold over upon the Altar. If made of polished wood, the steps should have carpet securely fastened on the upper surface, so that the Priest may step firmly on them. When not required, they should be put out of sight, into some retired place.

ARTICLE III.—*The various Chapels, Side-Altars, &c.*

1. The *Side-Altar* (*minus*) should be 3 feet 6 inches high ; 6 feet 9 inches, or at least 6 feet long; and 3 feet wide. There should be a predella or platform projecting 3 feet from the front of the Altar, and 6 inches, or at most 9 inches, at each side beyond the end. There should be no holes or cupboards in which things might be put.—*Gav.* According to the Ceremonial of Bishops, the Side-Altars are to be adorned with antependia, as the High Altar ; each is to have at least two candlesticks furnished with wax candles, and a Cross in the centre ; and the steps to them are to be covered with carpet, or at least with baize (book i. chap. xii. n. 16). Before each Side-Altar there should be a lamp, which is to continue burning at least during the times of Mass and Vespers on the principal feasts.—*Ibid.* n. 17. On the Side-Altars (that of the Blessed Sacrament excepted) there should be one step of wood, of the length of the Altar, on which the candlesticks and Cross are to be placed. —*Gav. and others.* There should be no stand or pedestal in the centre for the Cross to be placed upon.—*Gav.*

Each Altar should be furnished as the High Altar, with

Altar-cloths, Altar-cards, Altar-cover, small Credence or
Piscina on the Epistle side, bell, &c.

2. The *Altar of the Blessed Sacrament* is to be adorned
in a more costly manner than the others.—*Cær. Ep.* It is
an error to suppose that the antependium need always be
white. Concerning the antependium, *all* authorities agree
that it should be of the colour of the day. As to the Tabernacle veil, but one Rubrician (Baruffaldi) holds that it should
be always white. It is the *cover of the ciborium within the
Tabernacle* which is white or gold, and which does not vary.
According to the common opinion of the greater number of
authors, when the antependium of the Altar is black, the
veil of the Tabernacle should be purple ; such, says Catalani,
is the custom of all well-ordered churches.[1]

Although the Ceremonial of Bishops requires that there
should be five lamps before the Altar of the Blessed Sacrament, yet, according to the Council of Westminster, it
suffices that one only is continually burning. The colour
of the glasses used in Rome is the ordinary white; red
glasses may be the proper colour under the Ambrosian and
some French rites, but it cannot be considered so under
the Roman. The Council of Westminster wishes the pecu-
liarities of foreign nations to be given up in favour of
Roman custom.—*Decree* xxvi. n. 5.

Upon the Altar of the Blessed Sacrament there should be
a small vessel of glass, crystal, or metal, with a cover of
the same material, in which the Priest may purify his fingers
after having given Communion out of Mass. It should be
large enough to contain about one-third of a pint of water,
and should be kept about half full, with a clean purificator
upon it. About once a week, according to circumstances,
the water should be poured into the piscina, and fresh
supplied.

On the subject of the Tabernacle, throne for Exposition,
steps, and other details properly belonging to the Altar of
the Blessed Sacrament, see the article next above. In cases

---

[1] In Rome, the Tabernacle is often covered with cloth of gold. It is
unnecessary to say that *red* is not used at Rome as the characteristic
colour of the Blessed Sacrament.

where the High Altar is that of the Blessed Sacrament, the remarks made in this present article will also in part apply to the preceding one. However many Tabernacles there may be in a church, it is only permitted to reserve the Most Holy at one Altar at the same time.[1]

3. *The Altar of our Blessed Lady* is to have its antependium, not always of white, but of the colour of the feast. Blue is the colour generally considered appropriate to the Blessed Virgin, yet the Church has forbidden its use (in the place of white) for the Sacred vestments.—*S. C. R.* There seems no reason why blue should not be freely used in the decorations of the Sanctuary of our Lady, yet for the above reason it should not be introduced (at least to any great extent) in the embroideries on the Sacred ornaments. The flowers and decorations of this Altar may be, as much as possible, emblematical of our Blessed Lady; thus, the lily is peculiarly appropriate as the emblem of purity, &c.[2]

4. The *Image of Our Lady* is usually placed near, if not within, the Sanctuary. On Feasts of the Blessed Virgin, it may be adorned with drapery more or less costly; such is the practice at Rome with statues placed for devotional purposes. In the decoration of the image care and taste should be exercised; but it should not be overdone, or of a tawdry description, but simple, having regard more to the quality than the quantity. Candles and vases of flowers should not be placed too near the figure; if the bracket be not large enough to contain them, a small table may be placed beneath it, upon which all may be neatly disposed. Should a lamp hang before the image (which is most proper), it should be lighted at least at such times as the Faithful resort to the Church. Near the image there may be some chairs or convenient kneeling-boards; and, in a retired yet accessible place, a candle-stand upon which the Faithful may set up lighted candles as votive offerings.

---

[1] Sacratissimam Eucharistiam servandam esse in uno tantum Altari designando ab Episcopo.—*S. R. C.*, die 21 Julii, 1696.

[2] The Sacristan who is anxious to follow out the subject of flowers for the altars, will find a small pamphlet by Mr. Weale, called *Flores Ecclesiæ*, very useful. "The Catholic Florist," compiled by the same author, is a complete hand-book on the subject, with a view to the decorations of Altars.

D

This stand is usually of iron, painted; the upper part of triangular form, similar to that used at the Tenebræ Offices of Holy Week, capable of holding ten or more candles, according to local requirements. The base of the stand should be flat and of metal. A little dry sand sprinkled upon it will prevent any wax which may fall adhering to it.

The practice of placing an image of Our Lady upon a small credence or bracket within the Sanctuary, very near to an Altar at which Benediction is sometimes given, should be discouraged. There are but few chapels so small that some other place could not be found for it; however, where such must be the case, the image should be fitted with a veil, which may easily be drawn over it at the time of Exposition of the Most Holy Sacrament. The lights before the image (the lamp excepted) should not be left burning during the Solemn Exposition.—*S. C. R.* For the purpose of lighting and putting them out, a reed, with taper and extinguisher, should be ready near at hand. Of course, the above remarks are not to be extended to images which are merely those of ornament or part of the building. The distinction between those of the Saints, blessed for devotional purposes, and those which enter into the architecture of the building, is too obvious to need further mention. St. Charles recommends that the names of the Saints should be inscribed under the images less popularly known.

5. The *Picture of the Madonna* is, in Italy, often fitted with branch candlesticks, fastened to the two handles of the lower part of the frame, each branch holding one, or not more than two, candles. The candles may be lighted at times of especial devotion to Our Lady; but during times of Exposition of the Blessed Sacrament they should be extinguished, and if within a short distance of the Altar at which the Exposition is taking place, a veil should be drawn over the picture.—*S. C. R.* These remarks, as in the case of images, will refer to other devotional pictures, and not to those which merely ornament the building.

6. The *Pictures of the Way of the Cross* need not necessarily commence on the side of the Gospel, in order that the Indulgence may be gained: yet the Sacred Congrega-

tion of Indulgences (13th March, 1837) has recommended that, such being the custom and general practice, it should be adhered to. Each picture is to have the subject of the mystery of the particular station written up.

7. The *Baptistery.*—For matters relating to its construction, &c., the clergy are referred to the decrees of the Council of Westminster, pages 59 and 139, in which latter place are given rules from the Council of Milan, under Saint Charles Borromeo. The Sacristan will be careful to have everything required for Solemn Baptism ready for use. The cotton used in Baptism should not be left in the Font, but be destroyed after each occasion.—See *" Preparation for Solemn Baptism."* The cover of the Font, statue of Saint John the Baptist baptizing Christ, and other furniture and ornaments of the Baptistery, should be occasionally cleaned with a light brush. The keys of the Baptistery, and of the ambrey in which the Holy Oils are preserved, should be given up to the Priest, or kept by his direction in a safe place.

8. The *Confessionals.*—If that part appropriated to the Priest is under lock and key, the cotta and purple stole may be kept there, otherwise in the Sacristy. That part of the Confessional appropriated to the Penitents should have a kneeling-step below and an inclined board above, both so disposed as to allow the Penitent to kneel on both knees, and to have his hands joined. A small crucifix should hang before the Penitent (*Manuale Epis.*), and a suitable grating, 11 inches high, by 8 inches wide, intervene between him and the confessor. The latter should have the means of drawing either a curtain, or a sliding door across the grating as occasion may require. This is specially necessary when confessional openings are placed on each side of the Confessor. Under no pretext, whatever, may alms-boxes be placed in, or near to, the Confessionals.

9. The *Pulpit* should be so placed in the body of the Church, that the Preacher may be well seen and heard by the people ; yet, it should be as near as convenient to the High Altar. In parochial churches it is more properly placed on the Gospel side (*St. Charles*) ; but in cathedrals having a fixed Episcopal Throne, on the Epistle side.

If furnished with rich hangings, there may be a cover of more ordinary material, to protect them from dust. There should be black hangings ready for the occasion of a funeral discourse.—*Cær. Ep.* lib. ii. cap. xi. n. 10.

The Pulpit should be provided with a kneeling-stool and seat, the former so placed that the Preacher may kneel having his face turned toward the Altar.

10. The *Porch* is usually confided to the care of the Verger; nevertheless, the Sacristan will see that the Holy Water stoup, which should be placed within the outer door, on the right hand entering the Church (*Manuale Epis.*), is from time to time cleaned out and supplied with Holy Water. The boards on which the church notices are fixed will also require his attention, especially that one on which the mortuary bills are posted. Those bills should be removed as space is wanted, in the order of the time in which they were put up. The remarks in the preceding page will apply also to the type and characters in which all notices are printed or written, which should be plain and legible.

The key of the outer door should not be left in the lock, when the door is open, but be deposited in some safe place in the Sacristy. When the door is fastened, it is more prudent to leave the key in the lock. It is a good practice to let the door-mats, from time to time, be turned over at night, that the under surfaces may have some chance of becoming dry and sweet.

PART II.

GENERAL PREPARATIONS FOR THE DIVINE OFFICES.

ARTICLE I.—*For High Mass.*

1. IN the *Sacristy*, the vestments for the Celebrant and Sacred Ministers; namely, in the centre, the chasuble, stole, maniple, girdle, alb, and amice; on the right hand for the Deacon, the dalmatic, stole, maniple, girdle, alb, and amice; and on the left for the Subdeacon, the tunic, maniple, girdle, alb, and amice. If the office of the Subdeacon be taken by a simple Clerk not yet in Holy Orders, he does not use the maniple. A pincushion will be placed conveniently for the Celebrant and Ministers.

Note.—Should the *Asperges* precede the High Mass, instead of the Celebrant's chasuble, the cope will be extended, and the three maniples, together with the chasuble, placed on the seat in the Sanctuary.

2. The Acolytes' candlesticks will be placed on the floor, at a moderate distance behind where the Deacon and Subdeacons vest; a cotta, and stole of the colour of the day for the Preacher; cottas for the Acolytes, Thurifer, Torchbearers, and other assistants in convenient places. Should there be an outer Sacristy, they should be assumed there. *Priests*, however, will vest in their cottas in the inner Sacristy.

3. The thurible, boat with incense, fire and small tongs, torches for the Elevation, in number according to the feast, holy water, and aspersory, if required for the Asperges.

Note.—For the blessing of water, which takes place generally in the Sacristy on all Sundays of the year, except on Easter and Whit Sundays, there will be required a cotta and purple stole for the Priest; cotta and lighted candle for the Assistant; upon a credence covered with white a small quantity of salt in a covered vase, and the required number of vessels filled with fresh spring water; the empty holy-water vase with aspersory; a missal or ritual; and a towel. The Priest about to celebrate the Mass will sometimes bless the water after having taken his alb, but in this case he will wear the stole of the Mass.—*Gav.*

4. The *Altar* may be adorned with reliquaries and flowers according to the festival. The veil of the Tabernacle (if the Most Holy be present), and the antependium, if not already arranged, should be of the appropriate colour. The cover of the Altar will be removed, and the Altar-cards, more or less costly according to the occasion, set up in their respective places. The cushion, or bookstand, covered with a veil of suitable colour, is placed at the Epistle corner, having upon it the Missal open at the Mass to be sung, with markers in other places required. The Missal may also have a cover of the colour of the Mass, unless indeed the binding itself is highly ornamented. The candlesticks will, of course, be duly furnished with white wax candles. Should it be the duty of the Sacristan, he will first light those on the Gospel side, beginning with that one nearest the Cross; afterwards he continues with those on the Epistle side, commencing as before with the one nearest the Cross: they are extinguished precisely in a contrary order, commencing on the Epistle side with the one furthest re-moved from the Cross.[1]

5. The *Credence* for High Mass should be covered with a linen cloth, hanging on all sides down to the ground; it should not be adorned with Cross, images, flowers, &c. The chalice will be placed in the centre, the opening of the burse being towards the wall; on the right nearest the Altar, the cruets of wine and water on their stand, and a towel or napkin for the fingers; on the left, the Book of Epistles and Gospels, with the marker in the place for the day; and in convenient places (leaving room for the Acolytes'

---

[1] Whether the Preacher delivers his sermon from the Altar or the Pulpit, the candles should not be extinguished.—*Manuale Epis.*

candlesticks on either side), the communion-cloth, ciborium with particles, if required, and the small bell : the whole are covered with the humeral veil. The thurible with its boat, where it is customary to have lighted charcoal in the choir, and the torches for the Elevation, if not brought during Mass from the Sacristy, are also to be placed on or the credence.

6. The seat for the Celebrant and Sacred Ministers, which should be a bench about seven feet long, should be covered with its proper baize cover; green for ordinary occasions, and purple when the vestments are purple. Where it is customary to use a light lectern for the Epistle . and Gospel, it should be covered with hangings of colour and richness according to the occasion ; so also the steps to the Altar with an appropriate carpet.—*Cær. Ep.* The use of kneeling-cushions is reserved to Bishops.—*S. C. R.* March 24, 1612.

7. Should the *Asperges* take place before Mass, the chasuble will be placed upon the middle of the seat, folded in such a manner that the Sacred Ministers may easily vest the Celebrant with it as he stands, having his face turned towards the Altar ; the Celebrant's maniple on the chasuble, and those for the Ministers one on either side.

ARTICLE II.—*Mass sung without Deacon and Subdeacon.*

8. In the *Sacristy*, the vestments for the Celebrant as at No. 1 above ; the cottas for the Acolytes and other assistants ; the usual preparations for the blessing of water as at No. 3, page 35 ; and the torches for the Elevation. In these Masses the use of incense is forbidden (*S. C. R.*), and the Acolytes' candles are not required.—*Baldeschi.*

9. The *Altar* should be adorned and furnished precisely as at No. 4, page 38. The chalice will be arranged on an extended corporal in the centre, and the ciborium with particles (if required) behind it. The front fold of the corporal may not be turned back under the foot of the chalice. ,

10. The *Credence*, covered on all sides down to the ground, will have on it the cruets of wine and water on their stand, the towel for the fingers, the book of the Epistles

with the marker in the proper place, the communion-cloth
if required, the bell, and the torches for the Elevation, if it
is not customary to bring them from the Sacristy during
the Mass.

11. The seat of the Celebrant (except that for this Mass
it should be a stool or short bench), and the chasuble with
the maniple upon it, as at Nos. 6 and 7, page 39. The steps
to the Altar should be covered with carpet more or less
ornamented according to the occasion. A lectern will not
be used for the Epistle, nor are seats required for the two
Acolytes, unless a sermon is to be given.

ARTICLE III.—High Mass for the Dead.

12. In the *Sacristy* the black vestments as in No. 1, page 1;
the cottas for the Acolytes, Thurifer, and other assistants;
and the thurible, boat, fire-tongs, and torches for the Elevation. Should there be a panegyric, the Preacher will not
assume a cotta, but preach, being in his ordinary black
ecclesiastical dress.—*Cær. Ep.* In Roman practice he would
retain the *ferraiulo.* Incense is used at the Offertory, at
the Elevation, and at the Absolution after Mass, or after
the Sermon, should one intervene.

13. The *Altar* should be furnished with six candles of unbleached wax, and the Cross; there should be no images or
other festive ornaments.—*Cær. Ep.* The antependium
should be black, and have no figures emblematical of death
worked on it.—*Merati.* If the Tabernacle contain the most
Holy Sacrament (which should be removed if possible), the
veil will be purple. The Altar-cards will be of a plain
description, and the Missal, with black cover (open at the
Mass for the Dead), on a cushion or stand veiled with black,
will be placed at the Epistle corner.

14. The *Credence* should be covered with white linen,
hanging but a short distance over the sides; the chalice
and appurtenances in the centre; the cruets of wine and
water, with the stand and napkin, on the right, the Book of
Epistles, &c., on the left; the Acolytes' candlesticks, furnished with candles of unbleached wax, on either side; the
candles to be distributed to those in the choir; the bell and

communion-cloth (if required) in convenient places. The humeral veil is not used. The thurible with its boat, where it is customary to have lighted charcoal in the choir, and the Torches for the Elevation, if not brought during Mass from the Sacristy, are also to be placed on or near the credence. Should there be an Absolution given after Mass, the Holy Water and aspersory, a cope for the Celebrant, and a Ritual will be required.

15. The seat or bench for the Sacred Ministers should be uncovered (*Cær. Ep.*); also the steps to the Altar uncovered; but the predella should be furnished with purple (*Baldeschi*) or black (*Cær. Ep.*) carpet. The lectern, if used for the Epistle and Gospel, will have no hangings. The Processional Cross for the Absolution after Mass should be placed near the credence.

16. The catafalque may be prepared in the centre of the Church or in the usual place, and should be surrounded by lights; should there be a panegyric, the pulpit will be hung with black drapery.—*Cær. Ep.*

17. Should the Sacristan be requested, he will hold himself in readiness to distribute lighted candles to those in the choir a little previous to the Gospel.

ARTICLE IV.—*Low Mass.*

18. In the *Sacristy*, the Celebrant's vestments of the colour of the Mass;[1] the chalice and its appurtenances, including the key of the Tabernacle; the ciborium and particles if required; the Missal, if not already placed upon the Altar, and a cotta for the server. Two servers are not allowed by the Sacred Congregation, unless to a Bishop.

19. The *Altar* may be adorned in a more simple manner than for High Mass; nevertheless, a due regard should be paid to the various seasons of the Church. The veil of the Tabernacle and the antependium, will be of the proper

---

[1] The Priest may not receive his vestments from the Altar; where there is no Sacristy that he may use, he should receive them from a table in the Sanctuary.—*S. C. R.*, July 7, 1612.

colour, and the steps to the Altar covered with suitable carpet. On the Epistle corner of the Altar will be placed the
cushion or bookstand, and on it the Missal, closed, with the
edges toward the Cross ; at least, where it is not customary
for the server to bring the book with him from the Sacristy.
Two candles will be lighted ; namely, those at the corners of
the lowest step on the Altar. The Sacred Congregation of
Rites prohibits the use of more than two candles at a Low
Mass, to any under the Episcopal dignity.—*S.C.R., August* 7,
1697. A greater number of lights are, nevertheless, allowed
on account of relics which may be exposed, or the occasion
of some great selemnity. Cushions for kneeling, as before
remarked, are also disallowed, except to bishops.—*Ibid.*
Where the Priest is to duplicate, *i.e.*, say a second Mass,
a small vessel and a purificator should be prepared for the
ablutions of the first Mass. The communion-cloth may
be attached to the rails, if the Faithful are to understand
that they may there present themselves for Holy Communion.

20. *On the Credence,* the cruets of wine and water on their
stand, the towel for the fingers, the bell, and the communion-
cloth if required, and not already attached to the rails of the
Sanctuary.

ARTICLE V.—*Pontifical High Mass by a Bishop in his own Diocese.*

Note.—In preparing for the more elaborate functions,
the Sacristan will bear in mind that the work will most
likely be more quickly and efficiently done by placing himself unreservedly under the direction of the Master of
Ceremonies appointed to conduct them ; where, however,
such direction may not be had in time, he will proceed as
follows :—

22. The *Altar* at which the Bishop is to celebrate will be
adorned according to the solemnity. A seventh candle
should be placed behind the Cross ; it will be a little higher
than the others.—*Cær. Ep.* In the centre of the Altar, the
episcopal vestments in the following order :—Chasuble, dalmatic, tunic, cope (extended), stole, pectoral Cross, girdle,

alb, amice, and the gloves on a silver salver; the whole will
be covered with the Gremial veil. At the Gospel corner,
the costly mitre; and at the Epistle corner, the plain one
—each on its stand, with ribbons hanging a little over the
Antependium. If required, the instrument of the pax, with
a small napkin, should be placed near the centre of the
Altar, but behind. The Altar-cards will be removed, and a
canon opened in the centre. The Blessed Sacrament should,
if possible, be removed; if, however, it repose there, the
Tabernacle will be veiled. An antependium of more than
ordinary costliness should be used.

Should the Bishop vest in some Chapel or in the Sacristy,
and proceed to the Altar in Solemn Procession, the Episcopal vestments, as well as the cope of the Assistant Priest
and the maniples of the Deacon and Subdeacon, will be
prepared there. The Processional cross will also be in
readiness.

Note.—On occasions when *Terce* is not sung, the cope
will be omitted.

23. The *Throne* will be prepared according to the directions given at page 29, No. 20. The crosier and a kneeling-
cushion will be near at hand, as also a stand for the Archbishop's Cross, if required. The steps to the Altar and
throne will be covered with carpeting, more or less ornamented.

24. The *Credence*, covered with linen to the ground, will
contain the chalice and its appurtenances; the cruets of wine
and water; the ewer of water, basin, and towel on a silver
plate, for the Bishop's hand; the Missal, with the Bishop's
maniple, in the place of the Gospel of the day; the Book of
Epistles and Gospels marked; the sandals and buskins on a
salver; a cushion, or bookstand veiled; the Acolytes' candlesticks; the small bell; the thurible and boat, if it is customary to have the lighted charcoal in the Sanctuary; and
a small vessel for the pregustation.

25. Near the Throne on the Bishop's Credence, which
will be covered with white, will be duly prepared—the
bugia, a silver salver for the zucchetto, a Missal with the
markers in the proper places, and the Canon. On the *Bench*

of the Ministers,[1] or in some convenient place, their vestments; viz., maniples, dalmatic, and tunic, stole for the Deacon, girdles, albs, and amices. In any case their maniples should be ready in the place at which the Bishop is vested. At the seats of the Canons, their vestments, copes, chasubles, &c., according to their custom. In some convenient place near at hand, the amice and cope for the Assistant Priest, and the amices and dalmatics for the Assistant Deacons to the Throne. Seats will be prepared near to the throne, yet in a retired position, for the Clerks of the Book, Bugia, Mitre, Crosier, and Gremial Veil, unless, indeed, it is customary for them to sit on the steps of the Throne or Altar. Two cushions, of appropriate colour, should be prepared; one may be placed near the Throne, and the other on the centre of the lowest step of the Altar. It is forbidden to use the Missal cushions for kneeling purposes.—*S.C.R.*

26. Before the Altar of the Blessed Sacrament there should be a *prie-dieu*, or faldstool, covered with green or purple cloth, according to the occasion, having one cushion upon it, and another in front, upon which the Bishop will kneel. The Altar will be decorated, and six candles set up.

Note 1.—Should the Bishop make his preparation in the Sacristy, or elsewhere, the following will be prepared there: —the sandals and buskins; book of preparation and bugia; ewer of water, basin, and towel; a chair and small carpet for the Bishop; and the vestments of the Deacon and Subdeacon, except the maniples.

Note 2.—When the Bishop is to be vested in a side chapel, or in the Sacristy, rather than at the High Altar at which he is to celebrate, the following will be required:—An Altar having Cross and candlesticks; upon the Altar, the Missal, and the vestments, &c., as at No. 22, page 43; a seat raised above the level of the floor, upon the Gospel side, for the Bishop; and benches for the Canons, according to the disposition of the place. The vestments given in No. 25,

---

[1] It is recommended to have their vestments prepared in some other place—the Sacristy, if there be an entrance from the Sanctuary.

above, for the Assistant Priest, Assistant Deacons, and Canons, as well as the maniples of the Deacon and Subdeacon ; the crosier, book, bugia, a Missal with the Bishop's maniple, the ewer of water, &c., the processional Cross, the Acolytes' candlesticks, a cushion at the foot of the Altar, and the thurible, boat, and fire, in a retired place.

ARTICLE VI.—*Pontifical High Mass by a Bishop not in his own Diocese.*

27. *In the Sacristy*, the usual vestments for the Deacon and Subdeacon, but without the maniples. In a convenient position a small carpet with a chair upon it. Also the canon and bugia, and the buskins and sandals.

28. The *Altar* precisely as at No. 22, page 42, with the exception of the cope, and the seventh candle, which is never required by a Bishop out of his own diocese.—*S.C.R.*

29. *On the Credence*, the Acolytes' candles, the chalice, &c., a Missal containing the Bishop's maniple in the place of the Gospel of the day, the Book of Epistles and Gospels, the stand or cushion, cruets of wine and water, small bell, amice, and cope for the Assistant Priest, the maniples of the Ministers, a basin and ewer of water, two towels, and the thurible and incense boat. Near at hand lighted charcoal and the torches for the Elevation.

30. The throne is not required, unless for a Cardinal, Legate, or dignitary higher in rank than the Bishop of the Diocese. A faldstool will be prepared, with hangings of the suitable colour and richness ; it will be placed where the Subdeacon usually sings the Epistle, upon a platform about 4 feet square, 6 inches high, and covered with carpeting. Near the faldstool, on the lowest step of the Altar, a cushion, a stool for the Assistant Priest, and the seat for the Deacon and Subdeacon, on the Epistle side, covered only if they be of titled dignity. That for the Assistant Priest should be nearest the Bishop ; on it are placed the cope and amice, and on the seat of the Ministers their maniples.

ARTICLE VII.—*Pontifical Mass for the Dead.*

31. In the *Sacristy*, the usual black vestments without maniples for the Deacon and Subdeacon. The torches, thurible, &c., as usual.

32. The *Altar* should be unadorned, have but six candles, of unbleached wax; a black antependium; and a canon in place of the Altar-cards. The Most Holy Sacrament should, if possible, be removed. On the centre, the Episcopal vestments, as at No. 22, page 42, except that the maniple will be placed with them: the gloves are not used. On the Epistle corner, the plain mitre, with the veil for the Clerk who is to carry it. The crosier will not be required.

33. The *Credence* will be covered with linen, hanging but a short way over the sides; on it the chalice, &c.; cruets of wine and water; candlesticks with candles of unbleached wax; plain ewer of water, basin, and towel; a canon, Missal, and book of Epistles and Gospels, each with the markers in the proper places; the bugia; Holy Water and aspersory; candles to be distributed in choir; a black cushion or veiled bookstand; and the small bell; an amice and black cope for the Assistant Priest, and two maniples for the Ministers.

34. The throne or faldstool will be prepared according to whether the Bishop is in his own diocese or not. For the throne, see No. 25, page 43, and for the faldstool, No. 30, page 45. The seats for the Ministers and their vestments as usual (see No. 25, page 43, and No. 30, page 45): the seats are uncovered. The steps to the Altar will also be uncovered; but the predella, the steps to the throne, or the platform under the faldstool, may be covered with carpet of plain mourning colour.—*Cær. Ep.* The processional Cross in a convenient place, and a cushion on the lowest step of the Altar. The catafalque will be prepared in the centre of the Church or in the usual place. At the head of it there should be a faldstool for the Bishop so placed that it may be opposite the Cross of the Subdeacon.

ARTICLE VIII.—*High Mass in presence of a Bishop in his own Diocese.*

35. In the *Sacristy*, the vestments, &c., precisely as at Notes No. 1, page 44, and 3, page 33. A seventh candle is not required.

36. The *Altar* adorned as at No. 4, page 33. Should the Bishop assist, not in cappa but in cope, the following will

be placed upon the centre of the Altar :—Cope (extended), stole, pectoral Cross, girdle, alb, and amice ; the instrument of the pax and small napkin, if required.

37. The *Credence* as at No. 5 above, and, in addition, the book, bugia, and the plate for the zucchetto.

38. The *Throne* will be adorned as usual. If the Bishop assist in cope, the crosier will be placed near it ; also a stand for the Archbishop's Cross, if required ; a cushion on the lower step of the Altar ; and a *genuflexorium*, or fald-stool, covered with the proper colour, in a retired place. The seat for the Celebrant and his Ministers as usual ; also, where customary, others for the Clerks ; the crosier, book, and bugia, near the throne, but, if possible, somewhat retired.

Note.—At High Mass for the Dead, the seat of the Bishop will be covered with a purple cloth, but not of silk.— *Cær. Ep.*

ARTICLE IX.—*A Bishop's Private Mass.*

39. In the *Sacristy*, cottas for the Chaplains and two Torch-bearers ; and, if it is customary to present Holy Water at the door of the church, the Holy Water and aspersory.

40. The *Altar* will be adorned according to the occasion. On the middle of it will be placed the Bishop's vestments ; namely, chasuble, stole, pectoral Cross, girdle, alb, and amice. At Masses for the Dead, the maniple is placed with the chasuble, but at other Masses it is laid apart at the Gospel side, or on the credence. On the greater feasts four candles will be lighted, but on less solemn occasions two will suffice. The Altar-cards should be removed ; and the canon placed in the centre. The Missal will be prepared in the Epistle corner.

Note.—When the Bishop wishes to celebrate at an Altar at which the Most Holy Sacrament is exposed, he will vest in the Sacristy or at a side-Altar.—*S. C. R.*

41. The *Credence* will be prepared as usual and have on it the chalice and its appurtenances, the cruets, &c. ; ewer of water, basin and towel; bugia and canon ; Missal and

cushion or stand; a silver plate for the zucchetto and the small bell, *and* (if required) the instrument of the *Pax*, with a small napkin. Near at hand, two torches, if required.

42. Before the Altar of the Holy Sacrament, as well as before that at which the Bishop is about to celebrate, a *prie-dieu*, &c., as at No. 26, page 44; no seat is required before it. Should there be no Torch-bearers, two large candelabra, with candles for the Elevation, should be placed at the angles of the steps, at a moderate distance from the Altar.

Article X.—*Solemn Vespers.*

43. In the *Sacristy* the following will be prepared :—The cotta and cope for the Officiant; cottas and copes for the Cope-men; cottas for the Acolytes and others; the Officiant's book, with the markers in the proper places; the Acolytes' candlesticks standing on the floor, as at the vesting for High Mass; and the thurible, boat with incense, and fire.

Note.—The Officiant does not wear the stole.—*S.C.R.* The copes will all be of the appropriate colour; those for the Cope-men (which vary in number according to the festival) being of plainer material than that for the Officiant.

44. The *Altar*, adorned with reliquaries and flowers according to the season, should have a Cross and six candles as for Mass; the Altar-cards are not required; the Altar-cover should remain on; and the veil of the Tabernacle and antependium will be of the colour of the feast. (See No. 12, page 27.)

Note.—Should Benediction of the Blessed Sacrament follow the vespers, branch candlesticks may be placed on the lower step, but nothing should stand upon the table of the Altar; in such cases, also, it is as well to omit the reliquaries, since they would have to be removed. A corporal should be spread upon the base of the throne of Exposition, and the Cross so arranged that it may easily be removed. Remarks on the white antependium and the

veil of the Tabernacle, required for Benediction, are given
at page 7.

45. On the Epistle side of the Sanctuary, a rather tall
stool for the Officiant (unless indeed he occupies the first
seat in the choir), and on the right of it, but a little
behind, a seat for the Master of Ceremonies : the former
should be covered with green or purple according to the
season. On each side before the Altar, for the Cope-men,
stools or benches, according to their number : the latter
may be covered with a plain green or purple baize. For the
Officiant, a light lectern, covered with suitable hangings,
should be placed before his seat, if apart from the choir
stalls.

Note.—Should Benediction of the Holy Sacrament follow,
it would be prudent to prepare and place on the credence,
before Vespers, all that will be required.

ARTICLE XI.—*Pontifical Vespers by a Bishop in his own Diocese.*

46. In the *Sacristy* there should be prepared the copes
for the Cope-men ; cottas for the Clergy and Assistants ;
thurible, fire, &c., as usual ; and the Holy Water and
aspersory.

47. The *Altar* is adorned as at No. 44, page 48. The Episcopal vestments are placed in the centre in the following
order :—Cope (extended), stole, pectoral Cross, girdle, alb,
and amice ; the costly mitre with the veil at the Gospel
corner, and the plain mitre at the Epistle corner ; the
seventh candle is not required, and the Holy Sacrament
should, if possible, be removed. The vestments will be
covered with a veil of the proper colour.

48. On the *Credence*, the Acolytes' candles, lighted, the
canon, choir-book (in lieu of which a Missal is sometimes
used), and bugia ; should Benediction of the Most Holy
Sacrament follow Vespers, an ewer of water, &c., for the
Bishop's hands, will be required.

49. The throne and seats for the assistants, steps of the
Altar, &c., as usual ; the vestments of the Canons at their
seats ; the cope and amice for the Assistant Priest, and the

E

amices and dalmatics for the Assistant Deacons, in a convenient place a little aside; the crosier near the throne, a cushion on the lowest step; and the *prie-dieu*, &c., at the chapel of the Holy Sacrament, as at No. 26, page 44. Seats should be placed before the Altar as at No. 45, page 49, and others for the Clerks and Masters of Ceremonies according to custom.

Note.—When the Bishop celebrates the second Vespers of a feast, or the first Vespers of a feast the High Mass of which he will not sing on the following day, the cope, dalmatics, and amices are not required for the Assistant Priest and Deacons. For an Archbishop's Cross a stand should be placed near the throne.

ARTICLE XII.—*Pontifical Vespers by a Bishop not in his own Diocese.*

50. The whole should be prepared as in the preceding article, with the following exceptions : Instead of the throne, the faldstool is placed as at No. 30, page 45 ; the crosier is not required : there will be neither Assistant Priest nor Deacons, and the Canons will not vest in copes. In some churches the Cope-men assume their copes at their seats in the Sanctuary, which should be prepared accordingly. The lectern is not required.

ARTICLE XIII.—*Solemn Vespers in presence of the Bishop in his own Diocese.*

51. In the *Sacristy* all is prepared as at No. 43, page 48, and in addition the Holy Water and aspersory.

52. The *Altar* as at No. 47, page 49, unless the Bishop assists in cappa and not in cope, in which case his vestments and mitres will not be required.

53. The *Credence* as at No. 48, page 49, with the exception of the choir-book, which is not required on this occasion.

54. The throne with seats for the assistants as usual ; a cushion on the lowest step ; the seats for the Officiant, Cope-men, and others, as at No. 45, page 49, except that only the Celebrant's should be covered; and the *prie-dieu*, &c., for the Bishop at the Altar of the Blessed Sacrament, as at page 44. If the Bishop assist in cope and mitre, the crosier

should be placed near the throne. If an Archbishop, a stand for his Cross should be provided as usual.

ARTICLE XIV.—*Confirmation.*

55. In the *Sacristy*, the amice, white stole and cope, mitre, and crosier for the Bishop; an ewer of water, basin, and towel for the Bishop's hands; the usual cottas for the assistants; and the book of the registration of confirmations, with pens and ink.

56. On the *Credence*, the Pontificale Romanum, bugia, the Holy Chrism, pieces of wool or linen in quantity according to the number to be confirmed, a vessel to put them in when used, slices of crumb of bread and lemon on a small plate, ewer of water, basin and towel for the Bishop's hands.

57. In the *Sanctuary*, the throne as usual if required, a faldstool covered with white hangings and white cushions. The rails of the Sanctuary, or a space beyond it, if necessary, should have a foot-board placed for the children to kneel upon: this should be of convenient height, otherwise the Bishop will be required to stoop. Beyond the rails benches should be arranged for those who are to be con firmed—the males on the Epistle side, and the females on that of the Gospel.

58. Should the Bishop take his vestments from the Altar, they will be laid upon it in due order, and the crosier be placed near at hand. The six candles on the Altar are to be lighted.

59. After the ceremony, the wool which has been used to wipe off the Chrism, is to be burnt; and the water in which the Bishop washed his hands, together with the crumb of bread, poured into the piscina.

ARTICLE XV.—*Solemn Baptism.*

60. In the *Sacristy* should be prepared a cotta and purple stole for the Priest;[1] a cotta for the assistant; the book for

---

[1] For the administration of the Sacraments, Canons must wear the surplice or cotta. *An canonicis usum cappæ habentibus liceat Sacramenta administrare cum solo rocheto, et deposita cappa?* Resp. *Sacramenta esse administranda cum superpellicio et stola, juxta Rituale Romanum.*—S. C. R., 7 Apr. 1832.

the registration of baptisms, with pen and ink; the vessel of salt, which, if not already blessed, should be dry, clean, and rolled fine; and the Rituale Romanum. The book and the vessel of salt will be carried by the server to the entrance of the Church where the ceremony commences.

61. At the *Font*, the oil of catechumens, and the Holy Chrism, with some small pieces of wool or linen; the baptismal water in the font, and the shell or vessel to pour it on the head of the baptized; a basin to receive this water (unless it passes away through a piscina); a linen cloth with which to wipe the head after baptism (*Bald.*); the white linen for a garment; a white stole; [1] crumb of bread, water and towel for the Priest's hands; and the lighted candle to be given to the baptized.—*Rit. Rom.*

Note.—After the ceremony, the water which has passed off from the head of the baptized, as well as that (together with the crumbs of bread) in which the Priest has washed his hands, is to be poured into the piscina; and the wool or linen with which the Holy Oils have been wiped off carefully burnt, and the ashes thrown into the piscina. When all have left the Baptistery, let the gates or doors be securely fastened.

ARTICLE XVI.—*The Marriage Ceremonies.*

62. In the *Sacristy* should be prepared a cotta and white stole for the Priest, a cotta for the server, the Ritual, Holy Water and aspersory, a small salver, upon which the ring will be placed when about to be blessed, and the book of registration, with pens and ink.

63. Should the married couple assist at Mass, they may be accommodated with kneeling-stools before the Altar, yet beyond the rails of the Sanctuary. In this case also,

---

[1] Two stoles should be used, not one of two colours, as Baruffaldi observes: "*Absit penuria illa (heu! quam sordida!) versipelles stolas adhibendi, duplicis nempe coloris, seu utraque parte varie coloratas, adeo ut repente de uno ad aliud ministerium transiens sacerdos, fit scenæ mutatio sine loci et rei diversitate, non alio modo, nisi stolam invertendo, et pannum subsutum pro vera facie demonstrando, seu suppeditando.*"

the Holy Water, with aspersory, will be left upon the Credence, as it is used towards the conclusion of the Mass.

ARTICLE XVII.—*The Churching of Women.*

64. In the *Sacristy* should be prepared a cotta and white stole for the Priest, a cotta for the server, the Ritual, Holy Water and aspersory, and as many lighted candles as there are persons to be churched.

ARTICLE XVIII.—*Funerals.*

65. The nature of the preparations will mainly depend upon the Divine Offices which are to be performed. For the Mass see page 40.

66. In the *Sacristy* should be prepared the Holy Water and aspersory; thurible, incense, and fire; the processional Cross; Acolytes' candlesticks furnished with candles of unbleached wax; cotta, black stole, and cope for the Priest; cottas for the servers; and the book of registration, &c.

67. In the *Church*, the bier upon which the coffin is to rest, surrounded by four or six large candelabra furnished with candles of unbleached wax; the torches or tapers to be held by those standing by, in a convenient place; the candles on the Altar of unbleached wax; and the pulpit, if a discourse is to be given, covered with black hangings.—*S. C. R.*, 14th June, 1845.

68. Bishops, Priests, and other Clerics, are each buried in vestments proper to their order. The sacred vestments should, strictly speaking, be of purple colour.[1] It is a custom in some dioceses for the various missions to send their vestments, when no longer fit for use, to the Vicar-General's office or elsewhere, to be laid up for the especial purpose of being used for the burial of Priests. Clerks not in Holy Orders should be buried in cassock, cotta, and birretta; and Laics, in the habits of any confraternity of

---

[1] By a decree dated 24th May, 1846, the Sacred Congregation of Rites has sanctioned the putting a chalice and paten in the hand of the Priest, as conformable to ancient custom.

which they may have been members. The bodies of the
Faithful are placed in the church with the feet towards the
Altar; but those of Priests with the head towards the Altar.
—*Rit. Rom.*

69. At the burial of infants who have died after baptism,
under seven years of age, the Priest should be vested in
cotta and white stole, and the Cross is carried without its
staff (*Rit. Rom.*), to denote that the time of the infant's
earthly pilgrimage has been short.—*Bar.* The candles
should be of white wax, and the bell rung in a festive
manner, not tolled at long intervals.—*Rit. Rom.*

Note.—But one Cross should be carried at a funeral.—
S. C. R. When the Clergy of several parishes assist at a
funeral, the Cross of the parish in which the body is buried
should be used. If the Chapter of a cathedral assist at a
funeral, the Cross of the Chapter will suffice for all members
of the Clergy, whether secular or regular.—*S. C. R.*,
April 11th, 1840.

ARTICLE XIX.—*Solemn Benediction of the Most Holy Sacrament.*

70. In the *Sacristy* there should be prepared, an amice,
alb, girdle, white stole, and cope for the Officiant; the usual
vestments for the Deacon and Subdeacon, except the
maniples; or, should there not be Sacred Ministers, a cotta
and white stole for the Priest who is to expose the Most
Holy Sacrament, cottas for the rest of the Clergy, the
thurible with fire, and boat of incense, and the torches, not
less than two, or more than eight (*Cærem. Ep.*), according
to the solemnity.

71. On the *Credence*, the humeral veil, book containing
the Prayers, the small bell, and, if necessary, the foot of
the Monstrance, covered with a white veil. By no means
should any of the above articles be placed on the steps of
the Altar.

72. The *Altar* should be adorned with candles (twelve at
least) and flowers, according to the occasion. The cross,
reliquaries, altar-cards, and altar-cover should be removed,
but not left exposed on the Credence. The Throne of Exposition may be surrounded at a moderate distance on

either side in front with the lights; a corporal should be extended on its base. A white burse, containing a corporal, and over it the key of the Tabernacle, may rest at the back of the Altar, in the centre. The veil of the Tabernacle and the antependium will be white. Should, however, the Benediction immediately follow Vespers, so that the Officiant and his assistants do not leave the Sanctuary, then the antependium and veil of the Tabernacle, of whatever colour they may be, need not be changed; and the Officiant will retain the cope which he has worn during Vespers, but receive a *white* humeral veil when about to impart the Benediction. Should the Officiant, however, retire from the Sanctuary, then the antependium and veil of the Tabernacle, if of any other colour, will be changed to white. Some remarks are made at page 7, on the subject of the antependium recommended for use on this occasion. In respect to the veil of the Tabernacle, where it is foreseen that it will require to be changed between the Vespers and Benediction, it would be as well to place a white one underneath that for Vespers, so that the latter would require merely to be taken away. It is not well to place the corporals which have been used at Mass on the Throne of Exposition.

73. The following Decree bears on the subject of the vestments of the assistants at Solemn Benediction:—"An ad deponendum SS. Sacramentum a suo eminentiori throno parari debent sacerdotes tres, unus scilicet amictu, alba, stola et pluviali, alii vero duo assistentes pluvialibus tantum super cottas; quorum dignior assistens deponat Ostensorium, quin utatur stola, quia est pluviali indutus?" *Resp.*—"Negative et ad mentem. Nempe vel duo assistentes sumere debere dalmaticam et tunicellam, vel alium sacerdotem cum cotta et stola ponere et deponere debere Ostensorium cum SS. Sacramento." (Die 17 Dec., 1785.)

74. Should a Bishop give the Benediction, he will be attended by Deacons of honour in Dalmatics. His mitre and crosier (if in his own diocese) will be ready in the Sacristy; a cushion on the lowest step of the Altar; and a silver plate for the zucchetto, conveniently for the Master of Ceremonies.

75. During the Benediction the principal doors of the church should be closed, on account of the danger of irreverence.—*S. C. R.*, 17th September, 1822.

ARTICLE XX.—*Benediction with the Ciborium.*

76. On the *Altar*, six candles (*at least*) should be prepared; also the burse, containing a corporal, and the key of the Tabernacle.

77. On the *Credence*, the humeral veil, book of prayers, and small bell.

78. In the *Sacristy*, cotta and white stole for the Officiant; cottas for the servers; the thurible, with fire and incense-boat; and two torches.

Note.—In some dioceses the Ordinary does not permit the Blessed Sacrament to be taken from the Tabernacle for this function, in which case the humeral veil and burse with corporal are not required.

ARTICLE XXI.—*The Forty Hours' Adoration.*

79. The picture or statue at the High Altar, and, if possible, the walls of the Sanctuary also, should be covered with rich hangings, care being taken that the decorations contain no historical or profane figures.—*Instr. Clement.*, n. 2.

80. The *Altar* should then be prepared with all possible splendour and neatness, without relics or statues of saints. Care will be taken that the flowers are quite clear of the lower parts of the candles. Many accidents have occurred from the circumstance of the candles burning down, and the flowers catching fire.

The Throne of Exposition will have a corporal spread on its base, and the altar-cards and Missal be prepared as usual. The antependium should be white, even if the Mass require a different colour.—*Instr. Clem.*

81. In the *Choir*, at one side of the Altar, a bench, covered with cloth of a suitable character, and on which will be placed white stoles, for the use of those Priests who come, from time to time, to adore.—*Bald.* The steps should be covered with rich carpeting.

82. On the *Credence*, besides the usual preparations for High Mass, a cope for the Celebrant, to correspond with the vestments; the book containing the proper prayers; the Monstrance, covered with a white veil; the Host, fixed in its crescent; and a stole for him who is to expose.

83. In the *Sacristy*, the usual vestments, &c., for High Mass, and, in convenient places, not too distant from the Sanctuary, the large and small processional canopies, the processional cross, two thuribles and incense-boats, lighted charcoal, candles and torches for the procession, book for the Cantors who sing the Litanies, and at least four lanterns containing candles, should the procession pass outside the church.

84. The Sacristan, with one or more assistants, will commence to light the whole of the candles prepared for the Exposition, during the Preface, so as to finish, if possible, before the Consecration.[1] At the end of Mass, the Missal, altar-cards, &c., will be removed from the Altar.

85. The Blessed Sacrament is reserved in a Tabernacle at another Altar, before which the usual lamps should burn. In Rome it is customary for four candles also to remain lighted, on this Altar, during the whole time of the Exposition.

86. At private Masses, during the Forty Hours' Exposition, the bells at all the altars should be silent; to prevent mistakes, therefore, they may be taken away. The Sacristy bell for Low Masses may be rung as usual.—*Clement. Instr.*

87. The preparations for the Mass *pro pace* will be as usual for a Solemn Mass, and the colour purple. It will not be celebrated at the altar of the Exposition, or at that on which the Blessed Sacrament is reserved in the Tabernacle.—*Clement. Instr.*

88. The preparations for the Mass of Deposition are as follows:—In the Sacristy and on the Credence the same things as for the first day, the Host in its crescent, and the Monstrance excepted. On the Altar, before Mass, the key of the Tabernacle, the book-stand, the altar-cards, and,

---

[1] Such is the rule given by Baldeschi, and the common practice at Rome.

where the custom exists, the Cross. The benches placed for those who adore should be removed, and all the candles upon the Altar lighted before the commencement of Mass.

During the whole time of the Exposition, the responsibilities of the Sacristan will be very serious. He should pay an occasional visit of inspection to the Altar; and, when necessary, prudently appoint a deputy in whose judgment he can place reliance.

PART III.

PREPARATIONS FOR THE VARIOUS SEASONS OF THE YEAR.

ARTICLE I.—*Advent and Christmas.*

1. THE Altars and other parts of the Church should be adorned in a simple manner.—*Cær. Ep.* The rule given by Gavantus and Castaldi for the altars is, that they may be adorned in a partially festive manner with flowers, images of the Saints, or Relics, placed between the candlesticks, on those days only when the Deacon and Subdeacon use purple dalmatic and tunic, and not when they use folded chasubles.

2. The folded chasubles are used on the four Sundays of Advent, except the third, called *Gaudete Sunday*, and the fourth, should it be the Vigil of Christmas, when purple dalmatic and tunic are substituted. The chasubles are usually folded outside, and not turned up underneath.

Note.—In small churches, where folded chasubles cannot be had, the Rubric of the Missal (part i. tit. xix. n. 7) allows the Deacon and Subdeacon to serve *in albis; i. e.*, the Deacon in alb, maniple, and stole; and the Subdeacon in alb and maniple. A decree of the Sacred Congregation of Rites, given September 11, 1847, especially for London, prohibits the use of dalmatics instead of folded chasubles, and recommends that, where the latter may not be had, the ceremonies be performed by a Priest without Sacred Ministers.

3. When preparing for the midnight Masses of Christmas, care should be taken that each Priest be supplied with a small vessel, of glass or silver, for the Ablutions, and an

extra purificator : they may be placed near the centre of the Altar, or upon the Credence.

4. In churches where the Divine Office is sung before and after the Midnight Mass, the following preparations will be made :—For the Matins before Mass, a lectern, with a book open at the lessons to be chanted ; on the Credence, a white or gold cope for the Officiant to assume for the ninth lesson (*Gav.*), and the Acolytes' candles ; near at hand the usual seats for the Cantors, and near them the white copes, which they also put on at the ninth lesson. For the Lauds, the white or gold cope for the Celebrant will be placed on the Credence during the Mass; the lectern veiled with white for the Officiant, in a retired place on the Epistle side ; and the reeds with tapers and extinguishers, with which the Acolytes will put out and light their candles as at Solemn Vespers.

5. The Priest and his Assistants will retire after Matins, and vest for Mass in the Sacristy. The Priest will vest in cope for Lauds, at the Epistle side of the Altar.—*Gav.* The six candles on the Altar, and the Acolytes' candles on the Credence, should be lighted before Matins ; others may be distributed about the choir.—*Cær. Ep.* Incense will be required at Lauds ; and if several Altars are to be incensed during the *Benedictus*, care should be taken that the candles on them are previously lighted, and the baize Altar-covers turned back.

Article II.—*The Feast of the Purification.*

6. In the *Sacristy*, the cope, stole, girdle, alb, and amice, for the Celebrant; the folded chasuble, stole, girdle, alb, and amice, for the Deacon ; and similar vestments for the Subdeacon, with the exception of the stole. These vestments will be purple. The usual cottas for the Servers will also be prepared.

7. The *Altar* will be arranged in a simple manner for Mass, with a purple antependium and veil of Tabernacle over white ones. It is not necessary that the Most Holy Sacrament should be removed for this function.—*Gav.*

8. Near the *Altar*, on the *Epistle side*, a small Credence

covered with linen, on which are the candles to be blessed, covered with a white veil.—*Mem. Rit.*

9. On the *Credence*, the chalice, cruets, &c., for Mass, covered with a purple humeral veil over one of white; the Holy Water and aspersory; the ewer of water, basin, towel, and crumb of bread, for the hands; the books for the Procession; and the large stole for the Deacon.

10. In a convenient place, the processional Cross; the thurible and boat, with burning charcoal and small tongs.

11. On the *Seat of the Sacred Ministers*, the vestments for Mass, namely, the chasuble, stole, and maniple, for the Celebrant; the dalmatic, stole, and maniple, for the Deacon; and the tunic and maniple for the Subdeacon—all of white, unless the feast fall on a privileged Sunday, in which case the Mass will not be in honour of the Blessed Virgin, and the colour will be purple.

12. Should the Bishop bless the candles, the Credence, on which are the candles, will be placed between his throne and the Altar. The Episcopal vestments, cope, &c., will be laid out upon the Altar, in the usual manner; and the gremial veil, books, bugia, ewer of water, basin, towel, plate for the zucchetto, and the faldstool and cushions placed in convenient places.

13. In small churches, where there are not 'Sacred Ministers, the vestments for the Deacon and Subdeacon, and the humeral veil, will of course not be prepared.

14. During the procession the Sacristan will, if it be not a privileged Sunday, remove the purple antependium and veil of the Tabernacle, which have been placed over those of another colour; he will also, in this case, remove the purple veil from the Credence, and the purple cover from the seat of the Sacred Ministers, which should then be covered with green. The table upon which the candles were placed to be blessed should be removed. At this time, also, he may place between the candlesticks vases of flowers, &c., which should have been prepared beforehand.

15. The candles to be blessed should be of white wax (*Cær. Ep.*), not sperm or composition; they should be placed upon a table, or, as Cavalieri says, if few in number, upon

the Altar itself. Those are not to be blessed which are in the hands of the Faithful.[1]

16. The blessed candles should only be distributed to the Faithful who are present, and are not to be sent to the absent, unless to the sick,[c] for whom the Sacristan will reserve a few.—*Gav.* The candles are to be lighted after, not before, they are distributed.—*Cær. Ep.* lib. ii. c. xvii. n. 5. During this procession, the bells of the church may be rung.—*Castald. Bar.* and others.

ARTICLE III.—*Lent.*

The following are the preparations for Ash Wednesday :—

17. In the *Sacristy* the purple vestments, &c., precisely as in No. 6, page 60.

18. The *Altar* should have no ornaments except the Cross, candles, antependium, and purple veil of the Tabernacle if the Blessed Sacrament cannot be removed to another Altar. On the Epistle side is placed the vessel of silver, or some other becoming material, containing the ashes, which should be covered until the commencement of the function, either with a purple veil or with its own cover.—*Mem. Rit.* The Missal, on its cushion or stand, and altar-cards will be put in their proper places.

19. On the *Credence*, in addition to the usual things for the Mass, the holy water and aspersory; and the ewer of water, basin, towel, crumb of bread; and large stole for the Deacon.

20. In a convenient place, the thurible with its boat, a grate with lighted charcoal, and a pair of tongs.

21. On the *Seat of the Sacred Ministers*, the purple chasuble and maniple for the Celebrant, and two other maniples for the Deacon and Subdeacon.

---

[1] Nullibi benedicendæ sunt candelæ, dum laicorum manibus tenentur, sed præfato loco locatæ, ut monet Conc. Med. iii. tit. de Sacramental.

[2] In festo Purificationis B.M.V. non distribuantur nisi præsentibus in ecclesia candelæ benedictæ, et ad ægrotos tantum mittantur.—*S. C. Epis.* anno 1581. Candelæ in die Purif. distribui tantum debent præsentibus, nullatenus absentibus, et ne quidem episcopo.—*S. C. R.*, 22 Sept. 1737.

22. Should the Bishop bless the ashes, his vestments will be prepared on the Altar, and the gremial veil, bugia, &c. (as in No. 12, page 61). Should one of the *Beneficiati* of the church be appointed to hold the vase of ashes whilst the Bishop blesses them, a folded purple chasuble may be prepared for him.

23. In small churches, where there are not Sacred Ministers, the usual preparations for them will be omitted.

24. The ashes are to be made of the palms blessed the preceding year.—*Rubr. Miss.* The Sacred Congregation of Rites has declared that they should be used in a dry state.[1] In the seventeenth century the custom was introduced into some religious orders of going to the houses of the Faithful to distribute the ashes. The Sacred Congregation, having been consulted on the subject, replied, that it was not permitted. The ashes may be distributed by a Priest after Mass ; but to leave them on the steps of the Sanctuary, in order that the people may help themselves, is a custom directly opposed to decrees of the Sacred Congregation of Rites.[2]

25. For the ornaments of the Altar on the Sundays in Lent, the rules given at page 59 (No. 1) should be followed. On the fourth, called *Lœtare Sunday*, the Sacred Ministers use the purple dalmatic and tunic.

26. Before the First Vespers of Passion Sunday, all the crosses, images of the saints, and pictures throughout the church, should be covered (*Cær. Ep.*) ; they remain veiled till Holy Saturday, even should the feast of the Patron Saint or of the Dedication of the Church occur.[3] The veils used for this purpose should be purple, having neither figures nor emblems of the Passion worked in them.—*Gav.* Remarks are made at page 34, on the difference to be observed between those images, &c., which have been blessed, and

---

[1] An Cineres, qui super capita fidelium imponuntur feria iv. Cinerum, debeant esse aqua maditi in modum luti ?— *Resp.* Cineres aridos esse debere, et in modum pulveris in Ecclesia universali (die 23 Maii, 1693).

[2] March 26th, 1639 ; March 16th, 1844.

[3] Imagines et cruces detegi non debent, etiamsi in hebdomada Passionis occurrat festum S. Titularis, aut Dedicationis Ecclesiæ.—*S. C. R.*; 16 Nov. 1649.

are set up for devotional purposes, and those which are mere ornaments of the building.

ARTICLE IV.—*Palm Sunday*.

27. In the *Sacristy*, the vestments, &c., as at No. 6, page 60. Also three amices, albs, girdles, maniples, purple stoles, and books for the three Deacons of the *Passion*.

28. On the *Altar*, which should be unadorned, the Cross, candles, altar-cards, Missal, purple antependium, and purple veil of the Tabernacle, if required. Where the custom exists, branches of olive or palm may be placed between the candlesticks.—*Mem. Rit. Bald.* and *Merati.*

29. Near the *Altar, on the Epistle side,* a credence covered with linen, upon which are the palms to be blessed, covered with a white veil.

30. On the *Gospel side of the Choir* three lecterns for the Passion.

31. On the *Credence* the articles given in No. 9, page 61, with the exception of the white humeral veil.

32. In a convenient place, the processional Cross, covered with a purple veil, to which is attached a purple riband, to tie a palm to the top of the Cross; also the thurible, incense, fire, and tongs.

33. On the *Bench of the Sacred Ministers,* the purple chasuble and maniple for the Celebrant.

34. Should the Bishop bless the palms, the Credence on which they are placed will stand between his throne and the Altar. The episcopal vestments will be laid in due order on the Altar, those for his assistants in convenient place; and the gremial veil, book, bugia, ewer of water, basin, towel, silver plate for the zucchetto, faldstool, and cushions, each in its appropriate place.

35. In churches where there are not Sacred Ministers, the vestments for Deacon and Subdeacon will not be required; nor, also, the vestments, lecterns, and books for the Deacons of the Passion.

36. Where the custom exists of ornamenting the palms by plaiting them, &c., some more elaborately prepared than others, should be set apart for the Celebrant and high orders of the Clergy.—*Cær. Ep.*

37. During the Distribution of the palms, the Sacristan (unless another person be appointed) will securely fasten one of the blessed palms to the top of the processional Cross, with a purple riband. This palm will eventually be placed in the Sacristy.—*Bar.* Should there' not be a probability that some palms may be obtained from the Faithful, a few may be carefully laid by for the ashes of the next Lent.

38. During the procession the Sacristan will remove the table on which the palms were placed.

ARTICLE V.—*The Tenebræ Offices of Wednesday, Holy Thursday, and Good Friday.*

39. At the *Altar*, purple carpeting, a purple antependium, cross, and six unbleached candles.

40. The triangular Candlestick, with fifteen candles of unbleached wax, is placed on the pavement where the Epistle is usually sung. An extinguisher on a rod will be placed near at hand. An uncovered lectern will be placed in the middle of the Choir for the lessons, and the Blessed Sacrament should be removed from the Altar.

41. Should the Bishop assist, for the second and third nights, the throne, seat, and floor will be removed ; he may, however, retain the use of a purple cushion (*Cærem. Ep.*). The faldstool will be required.

42. It should be observed that the antependium and carpeting for the steps of the Altar are only used on the first Tenebræ office, that of Wednesday evening ; on the two next evenings the Altar will be denuded of the cloths, and have on it only the Cross and six candlesticks (*ex materia obscura—Gav.*), furnished with unbleached candles. The same will be the case with all other Altars in the church, except that at which the Holy Sacrament reposes. The candlesticks should not be laid flat on the denuded Altars.

43. It is contrary to the rubric of the Ceremonial of Bishops to place a *white* candle as the uppermost one on the triangular stand. In places where unbleached candles cannot be procured, white ones may be coloured with ordinary gamboge.

44. It is recommended that, when the lights of the church are put out at the *Benedictus*, some few persons should be stationed at different parts of the church, with small lighted tapers, to prevent any disorder which might possibly arise. Where the church is lighted by gas, the supply need not necessarily be entirely cut off.

ARTICLE VI.—*Holy Thursday.*

45. In the *Sacristy* the white vestments for Solemn Mass; two purple stoles for the denuding of the Altars; a white tunic, alb, girdle, and amice for the Cross-bearer; the Acolytes' candles, two thuribles with their boats; lighted charcoal, and tongs; candles for the procession; and six or eight torches for the Elevation.

46. The *High Altar* will be adorned with the most precious ornaments; the white antependium and veil for the Tabernacle, should the Blessed Sacrament repose there, together with the Missal and altar-cards, should be prepared. The Cross of the Altar will be covered with a white veil, and the candles be of white wax.

47. On the *Credence*, the usual things necessary for High Mass; also a Chalice with pall and paten for the sepulchre; a white veil with a white silk riband; upon the paten to be used at Mass two large hosts; white stoles for the priests who are to communicate; a ciborium with particles; a communion cloth; the white cope for the Celebrant; and the wooden instrument to be used instead of the bell.

48. In a convenient place, the large and small processional canopies, and the processional cross covered with a purple veil.

49. On the *Altar of Repose*, a corporal spread out, the key of the urn, and near at hand the small steps, and rods and tapers.

50. Should the Bishop celebrate and consecrate the oils, the following will be prepared :—The white chasuble, dalmatic, tunic, stole, gloves, pectoral Cross; gremial veil, amice, alb, girdle, mitres, and crosier; the cope, &c., for the Assistant Priest; dalmatics for Deacons to the throne; vestments for Deacon, Subdeacon, and the various orders

of clergy who are to assist; a Missal, enclosing a Bishop's maniple; the Pontificale on a table covered with linen; the canon and bugia; the faldstool; and the oils, balsam, &c., in the Sacristy.

51. In small churches where the Ritual of Benedict the Fourteenth only can be carried out, vestments for the Deacon and Subdeacon will not be required; nor also the second thurible and boat, stoles for Priests, &c.

Note.—As only the Altar at which the function takes place is mentioned above, it is necessary to state that the veil of the Crosses, and the ornaments of the side-Altars throughout the church, should be purple, and so fastened that they may be easily removed at the denudations.— *Bissus, Gav., and others.*

52. The *High Altar* is decorated in white, by reason of the solemnity of the Mass : if, therefore, before the solemn function, any of the Divine Office is publicly recited, the white antependium and other ornaments of the Altar should be covered with purple ones, to be removed before the High Mass commences.—*Gav.*

53. The *Chapel of the Sepulchre,* which should be within the church, and quite distinct from the Altar at which the High Mass is celebrated (*Merati*), may not have black hangings, either within or without.[1] If there be a large crucifix, the veil with which is is covered should not cover also the Holy Sacrament.[2]

54. The Sacred Host is not to be exposed, but placed in an urn (*capsula*).—*Rubr. Miss.* In Rome this urn is gilt, in shape like a sarcophagus, the door opening in front, not on the top. It is surrounded by lights, but not covered with a veil. That the candlesticks, vases of flowers, &c., may be disposed in order, a semicircular range of small steps, in the manner of an amphitheatre, is recommended

---

[1] Vetitum est adhibere quæcumque indumenta nigri coloris, ad ornatum sepulchri feriæ v. et vi. Majoris Hebdomadæ, tum intra tum extra locum sepulchri.—*S. R. C.* die 21 Jan. 1662.

[2] An liceat feria v. in Cœna Domini in Altari sacri sepulchri apponere velum album, quod e magna cruce descendens cooperiat Eucharistam?— *Resp.* Non licere.—*S.R.C.* die Aug. 1835.

to be placed above the Altar. These steps may be covered with white linen cloths, and the urn rest in the centre, not necessarily upon the highest step, but in a small recess of the width of two or three of the steps. The Altar should have six candles of white wax, but neither images nor relics of the saints (*Bald., Gav₁, and others*), although there may be figures of angels supporting candles.—*Merati.* An altar-stone is not required, nor more than one altar-cloth.—*Merati.*

55. A bench, suitably covered, and white stoles, should be prepared before the Altar of Repose, for the use of the Clergy who from time to time adore before the Most Holy Sacrament. Where such is the custom, benches may also be placed behind, for the use of the members of the confraternity.

56. For the Mandatum, a somewhat elevated bench, with a footboard, should be prepared in the customary place. Also on the Credence, the book of the Gospels, an ewer of water, basin, and towels for the hands of the Officiant ; a clean cloth with which he is girded ; and towels to wipe the feet. Near at hand there should be a vessel of tepid water, and a suitable basin. The Sacred Ministers vest in white dalmatic and tunic as for Mass, with the exception of the maniples, and the Officiant in amice, alb, girdle, purple stole, and purple cope. An Altar with Cross veiled with purple (*S. C. R.*) ; a bench for the Sacred Ministers ; the Acolytes' candles ; and the thurible, &c., will be prepared. *Merati*, and some others are of opinion that the ministers should wear their maniples. The Bishop would require plain mitre, faldstool, and cushions.

57. It may be further remarked, that the thirteen poor persons whose feet are to be washed should be dressed in white, and have the right foot uncovered.—*Cær. Ep.* *Thirteen* is the number according to the Roman custom, not *twelve*, which is the case in some French dioceses.

Article VII.—*Good Friday.*

58. In the *Sacristy*, black vestments for the Sacred Ministers, viz., two folded chasubles for the Deacon and Subdeacon, and the ordinary one for the Celebrant ; two

stoles, three maniples, albs, &c. A little apart, three albs, girdles, amices, black stoles, maniples, and books for the Deacons of the Passion. In a convenient place, two thuribles with boats, fire, and tongs.

59. The *Altar* will be unadorned; on it will be the ordinary candlesticks, with unbleached candles, not lighted, and a rather large crucifix veiled with black (*Gav.*, *Merati*), or purple (*Bald.*). The veil should be so arranged that it may easily be uncovered. The crucifix need not necessarily be of wood (*S. C. R.*, 12th Nov., 1831). The predella will not be covered with carpet; on the edge of it, three purple cushions will be placed—one in the centre, and the two others at some little distance on either side.

60. On the *Credence*, which should be covered with linen hanging a little over the sides, will be placed the cruets with plate and napkin; the Altar Missal, with uncovered stand or plain cushion; another Missal for the ministers; the Altar-cloth; the large black stole for the Deacon; a small vessel of water, and a purificator in case of need; the black burse containing a corporal, and upon it a purificator; the black veil for the chalice; the Acolytes' candles, unbleached and not lighted; the wooden instrument used instead of the bell, and a silver plate for the alms.

61. In a convenient place, the processional Cross veiled with purple.

62. On the *Gospel side of the Sanctuary* a long purple carpet, a long white veil, and a purple cushion, on which the crucifix will be placed; also three uncovered lecterns for the Passion.

63. On the *Epistle side*, the bench of the Sacred Ministers will be uncovered.

64. In the *Chapel of Repose*, the two processional canopies, the white humeral veil, candles and torches for the procession, the small steps; and on the Altar, the key of the urn, and a spread corporal.

65. In small churches the usual exceptions (see No. 51, page 67).

66. For the Bishop, should he celebrate, an uncovered faldstool, the canon and a purple cushion at the High Altar, and a white one at the Altar of Repose will be required.

67. When the Celebrant has uncovered the Cross, and placed it upon the cushion, the Sacristan will uncover all the crucifixes in the church, but not other images.—*Gav.*, *Bald.*, and others.

68. Towards the conclusion of the Adoration, the Sacristan (unless another person be appointed) will light the candles on the High Altar, and those of the Acolytes on the Credence. —*Gav.* He will then proceed to remove the benches which have been placed before the Altar of Repose. The procession having departed from the Chapel of Repose, the lights there should be extinguished; a few, however, excepted, if the Blessed Sacrament in the ciborium repose in the Tabernacle.

Article VIII.—*Holy Saturday.*

69. *In the Porch, or outside the principal door of the church*, a small table covered with linen, and on it the following:—A Missal and stand; on the Gospel side, as it were, a white dalmatic, stole, and maniple; on the Epistle side, a purple maniple, taper, and packet of matches. Near the table, the reed with triple candles; a small fire lighted from flint and steel, and the small tongs. The operation of twisting three long wax candles so that the stem shall have a cable-like appearance and the upper ends be separated each from the other, is not difficult to perform, if only precaution be taken to warm the candles previously very *gradually* in a *moderately* heated chamber.

Note.—In small churches, where there are not Sacred Ministers, the grains of incense, thurible, &c., and the holy water are prepared also in the porch.

70. At the *High Altar*, the cross and candlesticks with white candles; a purple antependium over a rich white one; and purple veil of the Tabernacle over a rich white one.

71. The *Bench of the Sacred Ministers* should be covered with purple over green. On it are placed—purple chasuble and maniple for the Celebrant, purple maniple for the Deacon, and a birretta for the Subdeacon.

72. On the *Gospel side of the Sanctuary*, a lectern, with rich white hangings, for the *Exultet;* somewhat nearer the

corner of the Altar, the Paschal candlestick and candle; near at hand, a stone or wooden stand to support the reed, bearing the triple candle; and, finally, near the entrance of the Choir, the lectern and book of the Prophecies.

73. On the *Credence*, everything usually required for High Mass, covered with a purple veil over a rich white one. Near the credence, the bell, and three purple cushions for the prostration.

74. In the *Sacristy*, purple vestments, namely, cope, stole, alb, girdle, and amice for the Celebrant; two folded chasubles, with albs, amices, and girdles for the Ministers, besides a stole for the Deacon. Beneath these, or in another place, by themselves, rich white vestments should be laid out for the High Mass. The following should be also in readiness:—empty thurible with boat of incense; holy water and aspersory (or at least water, salt, and the ritual, if the water is not already blessed); the five grains of incense upon a salver, the processional Cross, and the candlesticks of the Acolytes for the solemn Mass.

75. Near the *Baptistery*, a table covered with a cloth, the holy oils, basin, ewer of water, crumb of bread, slices of lemon, a sponge or rough cloth, a towel for the hands, a Missal, an empty holy-water vase and aspersory, a vessel to take holy water from the font. The baptismal water in the font should be poured into the piscina, and be replaced by pure water from the spring. A vessel will also be required, into which some Easter water may be put for the use of the Church, and for the Faithful to carry to their homes.

76. Should the Bishop celebrate, his throne will be prepared with white under purple; also, his vestments in convenient places—purple cope, &c., for blessing the fire; purple chasuble, &c., as at Mass for the Prophecies; purple cope for the benediction of the Font; and white precious vestments for the Mass. The basin and ewer, books, bugia, cushions, salver, &c., will be placed for the convenience of the Master of Ceremonies.

77. The side Altars throughout the church should each, like the High Altar, have two antependia, so fastened that the purple one may be easily removed at the conclusion of

the Litanies.—*Gav.* Should there not be a sufficient number of purple antependia, the side Altars may be furnished with white ones, even before the Offices commence. —*De Bralion*.

78. At the termination of the Litanies, the purple antependium and veil of the Tabernacle at the High Altar are removed, relics, images, or flowers placed upon the Altar, a rich carpet spread upon the steps, and the seat of the Sacred Ministers covered with green. At the same time (*Bald.*), or at the *Gloria in excelsis*,[1] the devotional images and pictures of the church are unveiled.

79. The Paschal candle should not be placed upon a bracket attached to the wall, but on a candelabrum, standing on the pavement at the Gospel corner of the Altar.[2] The custom of placing small candles round its base, to represent the Apostles, is an obsolete French custom.

80. The Paschal candle should be lighted at Solemn Mass and Vespers on Easter Sunday and the two following days; on the Saturday in Albis; and on all Sundays till the Ascension, on which day it is extinguished at the Gospel. Where the custom exists, it may be lighted at all the divine offices during Paschal time.—*S. C. R.*

ARTICLE IX.—*The Vigil of Pentecost.*

81. On this day Baptismal Water may be solemnly blessed in those churches where there are Fonts. It will be necessary to make the following preparations:—In the Sacristy, the vestments for the introductory ceremonies; namely, for the Celebrant, purple chasuble, stole, and maniple, alb, girdle, and amice; for the Deacon, purple folded chasuble, stole, maniple, alb, girdle, and amice; for the Subdeacon, as the Deacon, except the stole. On another press, a complete set of red vestments for the Mass; the Celebrant's in the centre, as usual. Lastly, the Acolytes' candles, thurible, &c.

---

[1] Velatas manere debere usque ad Hymnum Angelicum Sabbati Sancti, juxta alias decreta.—*S. R. C.* die 22 Jul. 1848.

[2] An cereus paschalis ponendus sit super candelabrum, vel super cornupium? *Resp.* Super distincto candelabro in plano posito a cornu Evangelii. *S. R. C.* die 4 Jun. 1845.

82. On the Credence, besides the usual things for Mass (the burse, &c., of red), the Paschal candle, and a purple cope for the Benediction of the Font; the whole to be covered with a red and then with a purple humeral veil. The processional Cross will be placed near at hand.

83. The Altar should have a purple antependium and veil of the Tabernacle, over red ones; an uncovered lectern and book for the Prophecies will be placed in the centre of the choir; and the seat of the Sacred Ministers be covered with purple over green.

84. Towards the end of the Litanies, the Celebrant retires with his Ministers to vest for Mass. The candles on the Altar are then lighted, and the purple ornaments removed. Flowers, &c., may also then be placed upon the Altar.

85. For the Benediction of the Font the preparations are given in No. 75, page 71.

ARTICLE X.—*The Feast of Corpus Christi.*

Should the procession take place after Vespers, the necessary preparations will be as follows :—

86. In the *Sacristy,* the cope, stole, girdle, alb, and amice for the Officiant; dalmatic, stole, &c., for the Deacon; and tunic, &c., for the Subdeacon. They do not wear maniples. Also, the Acolytes' candles, the processional Cross, and, according to the custom of the particular church, the sacred vestments for the Priests who are to participate in the ceremony, such as the copes, chasubles, and dalmatics, but without stoles and maniples.—*Baldeschi.*

87. In *convenient places,* the large and small processional canopies, two thuribles and boats with incense; fire and tongs, candles and torches for the procession, and at least four glazed lanterns, with candles, in case the procession should pass into the open air.

88. On the *Credence,* the white humeral veil, book of Prayers, and small bell.

89. On the *Altar,* which should be properly decorated, the burse with a corporal, and the key of the Tabernacle.

Should the Procession, according to the Roman Ritual

and Ceremonial of Bishops, take place immediately after Mass, the following will be required :—

90. In the *Sacristy*, the most costly white vestments for Solemn High Mass; the Acolytes' candles, &c., as usual; two thuribles and incense-boats; and six or eight torches.

91. The *Altar* should be richly ornamented, but without relics or images of the Saints. If there is to be an Exposition, a clean corporal will be extended on the throne above the Altar; the candles and vases neatly disposed upon steps, which may be covered with white linen; and the white antependium and veil of the Tabernacle (if the Holy Sacrament be in it) as precious as circumstances will allow.

92. On the *Credence*, in addition to the usual preparations for High Mass, there will be a white cope for the Celebrant; the Monstrance covered with a plain white veil; the Host fixed in its crescent; candles for distribution to those in choir; and the Processionale Romanum.

93. In a *convenient place*, the small and large canopies; near the credence, the Processional Cross; and near the door (should the procession pass into the open air), at least four glazed lanterns containing candles.—*Clement. Instr.*

94. The picture or statue at the High Altar, and, if possible, the walls of the Sanctuary, should be covered with draperies which contain no historical or profane figures. The way by which the procession is to pass should be decorated with becoming hangings and pictures: if long, small Altars may be erected at certain intervals. These should be ornamented with candles and flowers, but have no Cross. Benediction of the Most Holy Sacrament is not to be given at every Altar, but once or twice only during the procession;[1] in that case also a corporal will be required, and may be carried in a burse by a Clerk.

95. S.R.C. prohibuit ne pueri puellæque repræsentantes varia sanctorum martyria et mysteria aliquo modo admittantur in processionibus quæ fiunt in urbe infra hebdomadam Corporis Christi (5 Martii, 1667; et 7 Dec., 1844).

---

[1] Non toties pausatio fiat et benedictio elargiatur, quoties Altaria occurrant, sed semel, vel iterum, et altaria per viam extructa sint decenter ornata.—*S. R. C.* 23 Sept. 1820.

ARTICLE XI.—*Feast of All Saints, and Commemoration of the Dead.*

The preparations for the Second Vespers of All Saints and for the First Vespers for the Dead, which immediately follow, are as follows:—

96. In the *body of the Church*, the *Catafalque* covered with black cloth, surrounded by the large candlesticks furnished with unbleached candles.

97. At the *Altar*, a black antependium covered with a white one; also a purple veil of the Tabernacle covered with a white one.

98. On the *Credence*, the black cope for the Officiant.

99. The white ornaments of the Altar, together with any vases of flowers or relics, will be removed at the close of the Vespers of the Feast: also the white hangings from the lectern of the Officiant, and the carpet from the steps of the Altar. The Sacristan may light the candles of the *catafalque* towards the end of the Magnificat of the first Vespers.

ARTICLE XII.—*The Feasts of the Patron, and of the Dedication of the Church.*

100. On both occasions the preparations for solemn High Mass should be made as usual; the colour will be that of the Office.

101. On either of the feasts, should it occur in Passion week, the Crosses, images, and pictures of the Church, should remain covered (see No. 26, page 59). On the feast of the Dedication, the lights before the consecration Crosses on the wall, are to be lighted during the Divine Offices, even upon a day to which the office may have been transferred.[1]

---

[1] Accendenda sunt lumina ante cruces positas in parietibus, ea die ad quam transfertur celebratio officii Dedicationis Ecclesiæ.—*S. R. C.* die 28 Feb. 1682.

APPENDIX I.

FORMULÆ OF RULES WHICH MAY BE HUNG IN THE
SACRISTIES.

NO. I.—RULES FOR THE SACRISTIES.[1]

"Holiness becometh Thy House, O Lord."—Ps. xcii. 5.

1. The Inner Sacristy is exclusively for the Priests and their attendants, and the Outer Sacristy is for the Choirmen and boys.

2. Those who are appointed to assist in Choir will repair to the Outer Sacristy at the proper time. Having put on their cassocks and cottas, they may remain seated till the signal bell is sounded from the Inner Sacristy; they then stand in two lines, the juniors being nearest the entrance to the Church. When the Acolytes from the Inner Sacristy shall have passed through, the two lines will close, and proceed to Choir in processional order.

3. On the return to the Sacristy, the Choir will again form a double line, for the Priests and Attendants to pass through; they will return the Priest's salutation, or, if a Bishop, kneel to receive his blessing.

4. No member of the Choir, except him who fulfils the office of *Thurifer*, is allowed to leave the Choir, except by the direction of the Choir-master.

5. Strict silence is to be observed in the Inner Sacristy, except in case of necessary instructions, which are to be given *in a whisper*. In the Outer Sacristy, where silence is impracticable, all loud talking and other noise is to be carefully avoided.

6. There shall be two Masters of Ceremonies; one for

---

[1] See page 15, No. 48.

the Priests, and one for the Choir. The duty of the former will be to assist at the vesting in the Inner Sacristy, give the signal for forming the procession, &c.; of the latter, to attend the Choir in the Outer Sacristy, and see that the cassocks and cottas are *carefully* and *reverently* disposed of after the function.

7. No boys will be allowed to enter the Sacristy at the time of the Sacred Offices who are not usually engaged in serving or singing; and all the boys who attend (whether as singers or servers) are strictly to obey the Masters of Ceremonies and Sacristan, under pain of dismissal.

8. No females can be admitted into the Inner Sacristy, *on any plea whatever.*[1] They may speak, on particular business, to the Priests or Sacristan in the *Outer* Sacristy, but *as rarely and for as short a time as possible.* They are respectfully requested to observe these directions, with a view of preventing the necessity of enforcing them with any apparent severity.

(Signed)

——— $\left\{\begin{array}{l}\text{Priests of the}\\\text{Church.}\end{array}\right.$

NO. II. — DUTIES OF THE INNER SACRISTY.

"Holiness becometh Thy house, O Lord."—Ps. xcii. 5.

1. All those who are to assist at a function will repair to the Inner Sacristy one quarter of an hour before its commencement.

2. The duty of the First Master of Ceremonies is to superintend the whole *serving* department, and to be responsible for the *conduct* of those engaged in it, as well as

---

[1] Such is the rule at the *Gesu*, which, it is needless to say, is one of the best-regulated churches in Rome. So strict are they on this point, that the author was informed that it was excommunication for a female to intrude herself into the Sacristy; yet this might be accounted for by the Sacristies of the *Gesu* being considered part of the Religious House of the Jesuit Fathers.

The prudent Sacristan will be careful, when offerings of flowers, &c., are brought to the Sacristies for the use of the Altar, to receive them with affability and thanks, yet to avoid personal compliments, by looking upon these things in the light in which they should be given, as gifts to the Altar, or to our Blessed Lady, as the case may be.

for a due observance of the Sacred Ceremonies. He will remain in the Sacristy in attendance on the Priest and Sacred Ministers while vesting and unvesting, and touch the signal-bell when the vesting begins.

3. The Acolytes and Thurifer are to be in attendance in the *Inner* Sacristy at the vesting, and are not to quit it, on any plea whatever, *without leave* from the Master of Ceremonies. After the function, they will remain in the Inner Sacristy till the Priest and Attendants have unvested.

4. On the return from the function, the Priest and his immediate Attendants, with the Acolytes, &c., will *alone* enter the *Inner* Sacristy; and it is the duty of the Second Master of Ceremonies to close the door, so as to prevent the entrance of any one not authorized to be there.

5. When the Priest vests for Vespers or Benediction, the Cope-men or Assistants will also vest in the *Inner* Sacristy, and remain there in attendance.

6. The Server at a Low Mass is to be in readiness five minutes before the time appointed for the Mass to begin. It is his duty to wait on the Priest while vesting and un-vesting, and to assist at the Lavatory while the Priest washes his hands before and after Mass.

7. No boy will be allowed to serve with dirty hands, face, shoes, &c.

8. The Servers and other attendants, both in the Sanctuary and Sacristy, are to move about *briskly*, but with due regard to reverence.

9. No person is allowed to enter into the Priest's Confessional-rooms, except the Sacristan.

10. No Laic will remain seated in the Sacristy while a Priest is present, except with his permission.

By order of the Clergy.

NO. III.—RULES FOR THE SACRISTIES.

"*Before prayer prepare thy soul, and be not as a man that tempeth God.*"
Eccles. xviii. 23.

1. Strict silence is to be observed in the Sacristies, except a just cause presents itself, and then whispering only is permitted.

2. No lay person is allowed to remain in the Inner Sacristy, except the Priest's Master of Ceremonies, the Copemen, the Acolytes, Thurifer, and Servers at Low Masses.

3. It will be the duty of an Assistant Master of Ceremonies to attend to the members of the Choir and the Serving Boys.

4. The members of the Choir and Serving Boys will take their cassocks and cottas in an orderly and becoming manner. On returning from the church, they will replace them from whence they were taken.

5. The Assistant Master of Ceremonies has power to enforce the observance of silence, and the rules and regulations for the Choir, as given by Baldeschi.

6. All causes of complaint or appeals are to be referred to the Priest, who for the time being is the Principal Sacristan.

7. During the week, and in the absence of the Assistant Master of Ceremonies, the Sacristan has power to enforce the observance of the above rules.

By order of the Clergy.

NO. IV.—RULES OF THE CHOIR.

1. The Choir will assemble in the outer Sacristy one quarter of an hour before the time of High Mass or Vespers.

2. They will put on their cassocks and cottas in an orderly and reverential manner.

3. They will avoid speaking more than is necessary, and, when necessary, will speak as low as possible.

4. When the signal-bell sounds from the Inner Sacristy, they will arrange themselves in processional order, so as to proceed when the Celebrant leaves the Inner Sacristy.

5. No member of the Choir is to leave the church during the offices, except in cases of illness or by direction of the Choir-master.

6. The Choir will remember that, in the church, they are engaged directly and publicly in the Sacred Offices, and

shall accordingly take care not only to avoid scandal by any misbehaviour, but to conduct themselves in a manner befitting the house and solemn worship of Almighty God.

7. They are to observe the prescribed Ceremonies, and to obey the Master of Ceremonies without hesitation or reserve.

8. On their return to the Sacristy, they shall take off and put up their cassocks and cottas with reverence and care.

By order, &c.

Note.—To check the attendance of paid choristers, the plan adopted in merchants' offices may be recommended. There may be two books for signature,—the "punctual book," and the "late book." The former is dated and left out for signature. At a proper hour this is withdrawn, and the "late book" left out. In due time this also is withdrawn. Members whose signatures are found in the first book are counted as punctual in attendance; those in the second book, "late;" and those whose signatures are not found in either are counted "absent." One book is sufficient, if, at the proper time, a line is drawn across the page, so that signatures beneath it may count "late." Under this system there can be few disputes respecting payments, fines, &c.

APPENDIX II.

THE CARE TO BE TAKEN OF CHURCH FURNITURE, &c.

SAINT CHARLES BORROMEO drew up a set of instructions on the care to be taken of church furniture, linen, &c.; but so much depends upon the state of the climate and general atmosphere, that it is found impracticable to apply them to England. It will be easily understood that the linens and general decorations of Altars, and other parts of churches situated in London or large manufacturing towns, will

G

require to be more frequently washed and cleaned than those in country missions. We shall, however, give the few following general rules, extracted from Gavantus's "Abridgment of St. Charles," with the express recommendation that they be modified according to local circumstances :—

1. Twice each year, when the weather is fine, the Altars should be stripped after Mass, and left so until evening, that everything may have the advantage of fresh air. At the same time everything connected with the Altar (including beneath the predella, &c.) should be well cleaned.

2. The Tabernacle, Throne for Exposition, canopy above, and other things connected with the Altar, should be cleaned once each month.

3. The predella of the Altars at which Mass is said should be swept each day.

4. Candlesticks, crosses, thuribles, and other articles of metal, should, if possible, not be touched with the bare hands, but with a cloth. All stains, &c., should be removed before they are laid by ; and each should be put into a linen or calico bag.

5. Every six months the chalices and patens should be washed in water (with the use of soap and brush), then in two other waters. This should be done by one in Holy Orders, who will pour the water into the piscina.

6. Plated articles, which are always exposed, should be rubbed each week with a linen cloth, and washed in soap and water when requisite.

7. The glass lamps in constant use should be washed in hot water every fortnight.

8. The cruets, as well as the daily rinsing out, should be thoroughly cleansed every month, so that no incrustation be formed within them.

9. The upper cloth of each Altar should be changed once a month ; and the under ones four times each year.

10. The corporals should be changed after three weeks' use ; and the albs, girdles, amices, and towels, when necessary, according to the number of Clergy.

11. The purificators (of which each priest should use his

own) may be changed every eight days, or at most every fourteen days.

12. The cottas in general use should be changed when requisite : the towel of the Sacristy every week, which when damp, should be dried in the sun or at the fire ; the communion-cloths in daily use every fortnight; the larger ones every two months. On the greater solemnities all the linen should be perfectly clean.

13. Each day when the Masses are finished, the Altar-cloths should be covered after having been lightly brushed ; the dust should be well shaken out of the cover itself every week.

14. When the purificators and corporals are removed, they should be placed in a box kept especially for that purpose ; before being passed into the hands of laics to be made up, they should be washed first in soap and water, then in two other waters. This is to be done by one in Holy Orders, who will pour the ablutions into the piscina.

15. Albs and cottas having been washed, are to be plaited, or at least neatly folded ; corporals to be well starched and folded in the manner described at page 9. When perfectly dry, they should be laid by in their own especial place. It is recommended to place with them dried roses, lavender, or other flowers of the same kind, as well for the sake of fragrance and cleanliness, as to keep away insects.

16. Priests should not proceed to say Mass in soiled shoes or slippers ; there should be some pairs of shoes always ready in the Sacristy for their use ; also a brush, that when necessary they may clean their ordinary clothes before putting on vestments.

THE MANNER OF CLEANING CHURCH FURNITURE, ETC.

The following rules for cleaning church furniture, &c., are recommended as having stood the test of trial and experience :—

1. Lacquered brass-work does not require any rubbing, or the application of any powders or paste. It should simply be dusted with a soft cloth, or when, from the evaporation

caused by the presence of a large congregation, it becomes wet, wiped dry as soon as possible. Sometimes a little sweet oil, or a cloth, may be lightly rubbed on lacquered work.

2. Unlacquered brass is cleaned with polishing paste, and then rubbed well with wash-leather. If the article is very much tarnished, a drop or two of oil of vitriol in the paste will remove the discoloration. Oxalic acid and charcoal also make brass-work very brilliant; but this requires to be used sparingly, and not at frequent intervals.

3. The best method of cleaning brass plates on the doors of the Confessionals, &c., is to cut the size of the plate out of a large piece of pasteboard or millboard, and place it against the door, so as not to rub off the paint in cleaning the edges of the plate. Where paste is not required, rotten-stone or crocus and sweet oil are best adapted for the brass-work; but care should be taken not to leave any remaining in the letters, &c., than which nothing can look more slovenly.

4. Plated or silver-work is cleaned with whiting or rouge and spirits of wine, and afterwards polished with wash-leather, or when there is a plain surface, with the palm of the hand. It may often be washed with a brush and soap-and-water, but not where the water will get under enamel or jewels; sweet oil removes the burnt incense from plated or silver thuribles.

5. Gilt-work seldom requires anything but to be rubbed with a clean soft wash-leather.

6. Gilt wood-work is generally covered with parchment-size, and requires nothing but dusting with a soft brush or cloth. It may sometimes be washed with cold water and a soft flannel. Gold washes, for renovating gilding, are bad; they generally turn brown in a few weeks.

7. The practice of cleaning marble with muriatic acid, either pure or diluted, as occasion may require, is to be followed with caution. If too strong, it will deprive the marble of its polish, but which may be easily restored by the aid of a piece of felt, with some powder of putty or tripoli, and the use of water.

8. Alabaster is liable to become yellow, and is especially injured by the smoke of candles, dust, &c. It may be in

some measure restored by washing with soap-and-water, then with clear water, and a polishing with shave-grass. Grease spots may be removed by rubbing with talc-powder turpentine.

9. Encaustic tiles are cleaned with milk, and rubbed with dry coarse flannel.

10. Worked linen, Altar-cloths, &c., should be washed in lukewarm water with white soap. The best method hitherto discovered for taking ink-spots out of linen is, to dip the spotted part into melted tallow, and afterwards to wash it in the usual manner. The stains of wine may be taken out by holding the part in boiling milk.

11. Stains and marks may be taken from books by a solution of oxalic acid, citric acid, or tartaric acid. The operation is attended with little risk, and may be applied upon the paper and prints without fear of damage. These acids act upon common writing inks, but do not touch printing ink.

12. Wax may be removed from woollen stuffs by holding near it a live coal. Grease spots may be pretty generally taken out of silk or woollen cloth by being rubbed frequently with a piece of clean flannel dipped into spirits of turpentine.

13. Wax candles, when dirty or marked by the fingers, may be cleaned with a cloth damped with spirits of wine or turpentine. In lighting candles, the taper should be held to the side of the wick, and not over the top. Candles improve by keeping a few months.

APPENDIX III.

THE CULTIVATION OF FLOWERS IN ROOM-WINDOWS.

---

1. IT often happens that a considerable sum is laid out in the purchase of flowers in pots for some particular festival, and that the Sacristan is afterwards sorely perplexed to keep them in healthy bloom, even for a week or fortnight. The author will endeavour to lay down a few simple rules

for the management of flowers in room-windows, an occupation which will prove pleasing and innocent, and is calculated to give real enjoyment, especially in the pent-up city or smoky town.

2. The first thing is to secure proper plants for the purpose, for there are many which would defy the skill of the most experienced gardener to keep any length of time in health in such situations; a list of plants is therefore annexed; they are the most suitable for the purpose, may easily be obtained, and are not difficult to manage.

3. The three principal things requiring consideration are *light*, *air*, and *moisture*. Plants kept in windows naturally extend their branches and leaves to the light, and thereby become one-sided. It is wrong in practice and theory to endeavour to make them otherwise by frequently turning them, which not only weakens them, but spoils their appearance. It happens, moreover, that for the purposes of the Altar it is an advantage that they should form one good face or tier of healthy foliage. The plants may be placed as near the glass as possible; of course, windows having a south aspect possess the greatest advantage.

4. Plants in the window require judicious management as regards *air*. In *winter*, when plants are not growing, large supplies of air are not so important, enough being usually given by the room-door. As *spring* advances, increase the quantity, carefully guarding against the cold of mornings and evenings, or cutting winds; and if the plants are placed out in the middle of the days, they should be brought in before the chill of evening comes on. After the first or second week in May they may be set outside for the *summer*. Towards the end of September, or as soon as heavy cold rains occur, they should be placed again in their quarters for the winter, setting them out of doors when fine, or supplying them with plenty of air by the window, until the cold weather and decrease of moisture at their roots bring them to a state of comparative rest. It should be remembered in spring and autumn that the plants must not go out to-day, because they were placed out yesterday; the weather alone must determine. Sudden changes should by all means be avoided.

5. Judicious watering of plants in rooms is perhaps the most important feature in their management, and it is unfortunately in most cases ill-understood, being too often given mechanically, as it were, at stated times, whether required by the plants or not; and by a too eager desire for their welfare, they are frequented surfeited to death with water— in fact, "killed by kindness." In *winter* when the plants are not growing fast, keep them rather dry; in *spring* increase the quantity with their activity and the sun's power, keeping them in a medium state of moisture; in *summer* water daily, and in *autumn* decrease with the length of day and the returning torpidity of the plants until the dry state of winter is again reached. In spring and summer the plants should be allowed the full benefit of genial showers, which will do them more good than any artificial watering. Spring water should never be used where soft or rain-water can be had; the water also should always be about the same temperature as the air in which the plants are growing. In summer-time it should never be used cold from the spring or well, without having stood some time in the warm temperature. When in use in the Church water may be poured into the saucer, and not over the plant.

6. Judgment is required in stopping some plants at proper times, to induce hasty growths and increase the flowers. It is hardly necessary to mention the removal of decaying leaves and flowers : the latter are exhausting as well as unsightly. The services of a skilful gardener will be specially useful in the early spring. He will look over the stock, cut and train here and there, and re-pot where necessary.

7. Green-fly is apt to infest the young shoots or undersides of the leaves; to destroy them, the infected parts may be moistened, and dusted with Scotch snuff; or the insects may be brushed off with a feather. Fumigation with tobacco will also destroy them; and many Sacristans enjoy a quiet pipe.

8. The Sacristan who is intrusted with the purchase of flowers is recommended to apply to a respectable florist at least a month before they are wanted. In this way suitable articles will be obtained in pots properly drained and prepared for window-culture.

FLOWERS IN POTS.

For Spring.

Snowdrops
Early Tulips
Crocus
Narcissus
Hyacinths
Heartsease
Mimulus moschatus
Ranunculus
Anemone
Myrtle.

For Autumn.

Pelargoniums
Lobelias
Campanulas
Salvias
Hydrangea
Verbena
Fuchsias
Calceolarias.

For Summer.

Pelargoniums
Ten-week Stocks
China Roses
Double Wallflowers
Pinks
Carnations
Aloes
Annuals, as Memophila, Schizanthus, Collinsia, &c.
Myrtles, Heliotrope.

For Winter.

Chrysanthemums
Pelargoniums
Heliotrope
Myrtles
Fuschias
Aloes.

INDEX.

THE END.

THOMAS BOOKER, PRINTER, 53, NEW BOND STREET.

Ceremonial according to the Roman Rite. Translated

from the Italian of JOSEPH BALDESCHI, Master of Ceremonies of the Basilica of St. Peter at Rome, with the Pontifical Offices of a Bishop in his own Diocese, compiled from the "Cæremoniale Episcoporum"; to which are added various other Functions and copious explanatory Notes; the whole harmonized with the latest Decrees of the Sacred Congregation of Rites. By the Rev. J. D. HILARIUS DALE. 8vo. cloth, 6s..6d. A New Edition, with numerous additions.

Bible (The Holy), Translated from the Latin Vulgate,

diligently compared with the Hebrew, Greek, and other editions, in divers languages. The Old Testament, first published by the English College at Douay, A.D. 1609; and the New Testament, first published by the English College at Rheims, A.D. 1582. With annotations, references, and an historical and chronological Index. Published with the approbation of the Right Rev. Dr. Denvir, Bishop of Down and Connor. Beautifully printed in super royal 32mo. sprinkled edges, 2s. 6d.; or 3s. gilt edges.

The same edition, illustrated with eight beautiful Engravings from the best Masters, bound in French morocco, 5s., or calf, 6s. Turkey morocco, 6s. 6d., or extra gilt, 7s. 6d.

Moehler (John A., D.D.).—Symbolism; or, Exposition of

the Doctrinal Differences between Catholics and Protestants as evidenced by their Symbolical Writings. By JOHN A. MOEHLER, D.D. Translated from the German, with a Memoir of the Author, preceded by an Historical Sketch of the State of Protestantism and Catholicism in Germany for the last hundred years. By J. B. ROBERTSON, Esq. A new edition in 8vo. cloth, 8s.

Compitum; or, the Meeting of the Ways at the Catholic

Church. Books I., II., III., IV. Second edition, with additions; together with an Appendix, containing translations of the Greek, Latin, and other quotations. Small 8vo. cloth lettered, reduced to only 5s. per volume.

Church History (The) of England, from the Year 1500

to 1688, chiefly with regard to Catholics. By CHARLES DODD. With Notes, and a Continuation to the beginning of the present century. By the Rev. M. A. TIERNY, F.R.S., F.S.A. 5 vols., reduced to 8s. each, published at 12s. each, cloth.

Essays on Various Subjects. By His Eminence Cardinal

WISEMAN. 6 vols. 8vo. cloth lettered, £2. 2s.

"These admirable volumes will entertain, instruct, and edify Catholics wherever the English language is spoken."—*Tablet.*

Documents of Christian Perfection. Composed by the

Venerable and Famous Father PAUL, of St. Magdalen (Henry Heath), of the Seraphic Order of the Friars Minor at Douay, crowned with martyrdom at London, April 11th, 1643. Translated out of the Sixth and last Latin edition into English, published at Douay in 1674, and Illustrated with a Portrait of Father Paul. 18mo. 2s. 6d.

Flanagan (Rev. Thomas). A History of the Catholic
Church in England, from the first dawn of Christianity in this Island
to the Re-establishment of the Hierarchy in 1850. In 2 large vols.
8vo., containing upwards of 1,200 pages, 18s. cloth lettered.

This work is divided into two parts. The former, embracing the
period down to the Reformation, comprises the planting of Christianity
in England by means of the mission of St. Augustine and others; the
establishing of the Episcopate and independence of the Church, with
its relative attendant struggles; the foundation of the great religious
houses; the contest between Henry II. and St. Thomas à Becket; the
disturbance of religious unity by controversies among the Monastic
Orders, and the advantage thereof taken by Wickliffe and the Lollards;
the great schism in the Church; the Wars of the Roses and their con-
sequences. The second portion exhibits the state of the clergy in the
century prior to the Reformation; the prosperous condition of the
nation at the accession of Henry VIII.; the quarrel of that sovereign
with the Holy See; his assumption of spiritual supremacy; the con-
fiscation of Church property and progress of persecution of the Catholics;
the sanguinary reign of terror and penal enactments under Elizabeth
and her successor; the foundation of the English seminary at Douay.

Pagani (Rev. J. B., General of the Order of Charity).—
The Science of the Saints in Practice.
—— Vol. I., for January, February, and March.
—— Vol. II., for April, May, and June.
—— Vol. III., for July, August, and September.
—— Vol. IV., for October, November, and December. The four vols.
complete, cloth, 15s.
N.B.—Vols. II., III. (3s. 6d. each), and IV. (4s. 6d.) only can be had
separately.

Flowers of Heaven; or, the Examples of the Saints,
proposed to the Imitation of Christians. Translated from the French
of Abbé Orsini. Cloth, 2s. 6d.

Audin. History of the Life, Writings, and Doctrines of
Martin Luther. By J. V. Audin. Translated from the French by
William Turnbull, Esq. 2 vols. 8vo. cloth lettered, 10s.

The Life of Henry the Eighth, and History of the Schism
of England. By J. V. Audin. With Portraits. 8vo. cloth, 5s.

Dialogue of Comfort against Tribulation, made by the
virtuous, wise, and learned Sir Thomas More, some time Lord Chan-
cellor of England, which he wrote in the Tower of London, Anno 1534.
Crown 8vo. boards, 2s. 6d.

Charity (On) in Conversation. From the French of
R. Père Huguet, Marist. Cloth, 2s. 6d.

Twelve Lectures on the Connection between Science and
Revealed Religion, with Map and Plates. By Cardinal Wiseman.
Third edition, in 1 vol. small 8vo. cloth, reduced to 5s.

www.ingramcontent.com/pod-product-compliance
Lightning Source LLC
Chambersburg PA
CBHW020805020726
47495CB00008B/2605